All Stars Fall

Also from Rachel Van Dyken

Liars, Inc.
Dirty Exes

The Players Game Series
Fraternize
Infraction
MVP

The Consequence Series
The Consequence of Loving Colton
The Consequence of Revenge
The Consequence of Seduction
The Consequence of Rejection

The Wingmen Inc. Series
The Matchmaker's Playbook
The Matchmaker's Replacement

Curious Liaisons Series
Cheater
Cheater's Regret

The Bet Series
The Bet
The Wager
The Dare

The Ruin Series
Ruin
Toxic
Fearless
Shame

The Eagle Elite Series
Elite
Elect

Enamor
Entice
Elicit
Bang Bang
Enforce
Ember
Elude
Empire
Enrage
Eulogy
Envy

The Seaside Series
Tear
Pull
Shatter
Forever
Fall
Eternal
Strung
Capture

The Renwick House Series
The Ugly Duckling Debutante
The Seduction of Sebastian St. James
An Unlikely Alliance
The Redemption of Lord Rawlings
The Devil Duke Takes a Bride

The London Fairy Tales Series
Upon a Midnight Dream
Whispered Music
The Wolf's Pursuit
When Ash Falls

The Seasons of Paleo Series
Savage Winter
Feral Spring

The Wallflower Series (with Leah Sanders)
Waltzing with the Wallflower
Beguiling Bridget
Taming Wilde

The Dark Ones Saga
The Dark Ones
Untouchable Darkness
Dark Surrender
Darkest Temptation

Stand-Alones
Hurt: A Collection (with Kristin Vayden and Elyse Faber)
Rip
Compromising Kessen
Every Girl Does It
The Parting Gift (with Leah Sanders)
Divine Uprising

All Stars Fall

By Rachel Van Dyken

A Seaside Pictures/Big Sky Novella

Introduction by Kristen Proby

EVIL EYE
CONCEPTS

All Stars Fall: A Seaside Pictures/Big Sky Novella
By Rachel Van Dyken
Copyright 2019
ISBN: 978-1-970077-13-1

Published by Evil Eye Concepts, Incorporated

An Introduction to the Kristen Proby Crossover Collection

Everyone knows there's nothing I love more than a happy ending. It's what I do for a living–I'm in LOVE with love. And what's better than love? More love, of course!

Just imagine, Louis Vuitton and Tiffany, collaborating on the world's most perfect handbag. Jimmy Choo and Louboutin, making shoes just for me. Not loving it enough? What if Hugh Grant in *Notting Hill* was the man to barge into Sandra Bullock's office in *The Proposal?* I think we can all agree that Julia Roberts' character would have had her hands full with Ryan Reynolds.

Now imagine what would happen if one of the characters from my Big Sky Series met up with other characters from some of your favorite authors' series. Well, wonder no more because The Kristen Proby Crossover Collection is here, and I could not be more excited!

Rachel Van Dyken, Laura Kaye, Sawyer Bennett, Monica Murphy, Samantha Young, and K.L. Grayson are all bringing their own beloved characters to play – and find their happy endings – in my world. Can you imagine all the love, laughter and shenanigans in store?

I hope you enjoy the journey between worlds!

Love,
Kristen Proby

The Kristen Proby Crossover Collection features a new novel by Kristen Proby and six by some of her favorite writers:

Kristen Proby – Soaring with Fallon
Sawyer Bennett – Wicked Force
KL Grayson – Crazy Imperfect Love
Laura Kaye – Worth Fighting For
Monica Murphy – Nothing Without You
Rachel Van Dyken – All Stars Fall
Samantha Young – Hold On

Acknowledgments from the Author

This is always the hard part for me. I have so many people to thank and after writing a book you're kind of brain dead. I'm so thankful to God for being able to do what I love day in and day out, to my husband for putting up with my mood swings when I'm on deadline, my son for eating more chicken nuggets than a child should when I'm trying to finish a book or when I'm just starting. And Kristen, I have you in the middle here right after family because girl, you invited me into your family and let me do this crossover series with you, and I could not be more honored to be a part of this project. In fact, I want to pinch myself, I'm so thankful that you trusted me with your world and also didn't hate the story. You are such a talented author. I'm so thrilled to be a part of this! To the amazing Liz Berry, meeting you, working with you, has been an absolute dream come true. MJ Rose, thank you for your incredible marketing! Nina, the best publicist ever (truly) thanks for putting up with my daily crazy, and to my incredible readers. You are my family. Thank you for everything you do! Blood in, No out, hugs, RVD

Sign up for the 1001 Dark Nights Newsletter
and be entered to win a Tiffany Lock necklace.

There's a contest every quarter!

Go to www.1001DarkNights.com to subscribe.

As a bonus, all subscribers can download
FIVE FREE exclusive books!

Prologue

Trevor, May 2007

Adrenaline World Tour
Staples Center

"We sold out three nights in a row." Our manager Dick, who I often called Dick for other reasons, did a little jig in his cowboy boots. He was probably dreaming of dollar signs and prostitutes.

I gripped my drumsticks in my hands and waited for the crowd to die down. My only job was to keep the beat, sing, and look sexy with my shirt off.

Literally.

It was in my contract.

The same one Dick had been convinced was the best contract he'd ever seen. We were offered a ridiculous amount of money to do something we loved. We were living the teen dream.

Except it was getting really old.

We'd been on and off tour for eight years. I was pulled from middle school, never went to high school, and my first experience with drugs was at twelve.

Good times.

"Listen up, boys—"

Oh good, another speech. Because that was what a rowdy group of twenty-one-year-olds wanted. Lectures.

"I didn't want to say this before, but the record company wants another album."

I suppressed my groan, locking eyes with my bandmates; each of them paled a bit.

We just wanted to go home.

The problem was, we'd never really had one.

A tour bus.

That's what we called home.

We had enough money to buy shit. We just didn't have enough time to spend it or lay down roots.

Hell, staying home on a Saturday night sounded like gold.

"By your excited expressions I can tell we'll need to talk more." His voice was grim. He rubbed his hands together. "Get out there and kick some ass. And, Trevor?"

I stopped in my tracks and waited.

"We have a few groupies hanging backstage tonight—you need to be there, none of this 'I have a headache' bullshit. You're in this now, you know what your contract says. Play nice or don't play at all."

I'd heard it a million times.

I gave him a firm nod while flipping him off in my head and made my way on stage.

I was first. Always first. I played drums for half the time then swapped with Ty so that the girls could see my six pack and watch me croon into the microphone while sweat dripped off my chin.

Goals, right?

The screams were deafening, the lights so hot I was already sweating.

I held up both drumsticks in the air. And perfect silence ensued.

Boys pretending we were men, that's what we were.

With too much money. Too much power.

A bra found its way near my feet.

With a smirk I knelt down and picked it up with my drumstick, then flipped it back toward the crowd, my white T-shirt following like it always did, and I made the walk to my set.

The girls' screams pierced my ears as I sat and held my sticks high while the rest of my guys joined me on stage. We were the first boy band to actually play our own instruments. We did it all. Ty made his way on stage next, in nothing but ripped jeans and a red tank, ink covering his chest the way it swirled up and down my arms. And then there was Will, perfect golden boy Will, the product of movie-star good looks and a heart full of gold. He flashed his smile across the crowd, and Drew followed last. Always last, the brooder.

We each had our role.

God, I hated it.

We played our set.

And I realized then I'd lost something, something valuable. At twenty-one, I resented what had made me feel the most alive for my entire life—music.

I slammed my sticks over my thigh after our final song and made my way backstage, nearly colliding with a stagehand before barreling into a woman.

"Shit." I gripped her by the shoulders. "Sorry, I wasn't watching where—"

Her light blue eyes blinked up at me wide and expectant. Her short cropped jet black hair only made me stare harder. She was beautiful. And familiar. "Are you—"

"Josephine Shannon, but everyone calls me Josie." She held out her hand and smiled a confident smile I felt all the way to my toes.

Without a second thought, I grabbed her hand and pulled her against me. "Josephine Shannon, I'm going to marry you."

And just like that, my life clicked back into place.

Chapter One

Penelope

Present Day Seaside, Oregon

It was a mistake.

I didn't say it out loud, just thought it over and over again during my hellishly long drive from Cunningham Falls to Seaside, Oregon, of all places. My cousin Dani said it was a great place to relocate and that it was basically impossible to be depressed around a giant sandbox.

But the minute I stepped foot out of my car, I realized.

You can't just leave your past and pray it stays there. No, it follows just like baggage can't help but exist. I had no good reason to leave other than I felt like every single friend I had grown up with or met recently was finally settling down, it seemed like I was the only one still struggling to find my purpose, my adventure. It wasn't the best reason to move several states away but it was all I had.

I exhaled roughly as I took in my small beachside cottage near C Street right by one of the local coffee shops. They'd hired me without even meeting me, and the owner had been so thankful that I had experience being a barista that she said I could start right away. Apparently, she was taking her youngest to college and wanted to be there to get him settled in.

Which meant I had zero time to unpack my stuff. Luckily, I was two doors down so I parked my car, grabbed my purse, and made my way over to the small red and white building.

The door was open, a trend I was noticing in Seaside. Even though it was chilly with the breeze coming off the beach, the doors were always open as if begging people to come strolling in.

I frowned at the tattered screen and pulled open the door. A bell rang overhead. The shop was maybe eight hundred square feet. They had a brand new espresso machine behind the bar and two new MacBook Pros in the corner for customers. A flat screen was placed near a few tables and Judge Judy was playing in the background.

I tried to shove away the disappointment I felt.

I'd moved to find adventure.

And I guess to escape.

And now I was sitting in an empty coffee shop while Judge Judy yelled at some pimple-faced kid for breaking his mom's window and then suing her for physical harm.

"Hello?" I called out in a loud voice, hoping that Jennifer, the lady I'd talked to, would answer. "Hello?"

"She's not here," a voice said from behind the counter. I peeked around the corner. A girl who looked maybe fourteen popped her gum and stared down at her phone. "Went to Subway—likes their bread."

"Uh-huh." Seaside? Really? Why not Portland? Seattle? Boise? "I'll just wait for her then. I'm Penelope. I'm the new—"

The bell rang over the door.

I waited for the teen to get up.

If anything, she seemed even more concerned with her phone.

There was something vaguely familiar about the man that stepped up to the counter. "Have you ordered yet?"

"No." I waved him off. "Actually I'm supposed to start work here and—" I sent a glare toward the girl still sitting. "—you know what, I'll just help you, what do you want?"

His eyes raked over me briefly before he gave his head a shake. "Black coffee, three hot chocolates, and advice on how to get gum out of both real and synthetic hair." His smile was brilliantly white, movie-star level. What was a guy like him doing in Seaside? And I was officially staring a little too hard.

I ducked my head. Great. I just met a gorgeous, probably taken guy and I was willing to bet I smelled like potato chips and diet Coke, not to mention my makeup had completely melted off my face during the drive.

"I'm not sure about the gum, but I think I can help you with everything else." My voice came out more like a croak than something sexy or even remotely normal, just adding to the embarrassment and total panic now that I faced the machine.

Why had this been a good idea again?

The teen popped her gum behind me.

I gritted my teeth.

I could do this.

Easy.

Cake.

I'd done this a thousand times. I closed my eyes, exhaled, opened them again, and let myself default into barista mode.

Within five minutes, I had all his drinks and was staring down the oldest looking cash register I'd ever seen in my entire life.

Did the thing even work?

"Peanut butter." Surly teen said from behind me. "Really creamy peanut butter, get it up to the root and start pulling the gum away one hair at a time." She tapped against the register. "That'll be seven-fifty."

He handed her a ten, but locked eyes with me. "Keep the change."

She flashed him a bored smile, stuffed the extra change into the empty tip jar then walked slower than I thought physically possible back to her stool and slumped over her phone again.

Unbelievable.

The little bell on the door went off as he left and I found myself staring after the teen who still couldn't bring herself to acknowledge me.

"You're welcome," I found myself saying.

Her head didn't even lift. "Uh-huh."

That was it. When I had kids, no screen time! They got books and puzzles, nature!

You know, if I didn't repel men.

Or stare at them slack-jawed like I'd just done.

I was off to a solid start, wasn't I?

The bell rang, alerting me to another customer.

The lady's hair was pulled back into a sleek black ponytail. She had four cases of muffins in her hands and narrowed her eyes at me. "Penelope?"

"Oh, thank God, you must be Jennifer?"

"Yes!" she squealed, moving her feet and almost dropping the muffins. The woman looked like she'd stepped out of a yoga studio. You know the type, where their bodies just refuse to age past thirty-five. She looked like a total adult, the kind that even had the matching bra and panties just because she could.

I suddenly felt very insecure about my teal panties and black sports bra under my jersey tank.

I mean, you don't drive in expensive lingerie.

Not that I would know.

Since I didn't own any.

I chewed my lower lip.

"Did you just get in?" Jennifer asked, breaking my concentration.

"Yup." I rocked my weight back on the heels of my Nikes and shoved my hands in my pockets. "I must have gotten confused because I thought I was supposed to meet you today and—"

"Yes, totally my fault. I was stuck in traffic."

Here? I wanted to ask but kept my mouth shut.

"You'd think that we were the new 'it' spot with all the Hollywood sightings, but it's normal to us now, you know? Rock stars, actors, whatever, as long as they're a paying customer, I don't care." She scrunched up her nose.

Wait, what were we talking about?

I was clearly exhausted. "Hey, as long as they love coffee." That sounded normal, right? Not desperate?

She beamed at me, all white teeth and red lipstick. "I knew you would be a great fit." She peered around my body. "Stella, you can go now. Thanks for watching the shop."

Stella hopped off her stool, gave us a finger wave, and walked right out the front door.

"Is she—"

"Oh no, no, God, no." Jennifer laughed. "I have two boys. She's friends with Mark, the younger one, though she's even younger than him. I pay her exactly ten dollars to watch the store when I have to run errands and promise her peeks of his six pack."

I burst out laughing. "I'm sure it works every time."

"She asked to pay me once." Jennifer giggled. "Anyways, thanks again for all of this. I actually leave tomorrow, so let's go over everything and then I'll leave you alone to unpack."

"Great!" Was it though? Why did it feel like I was trading my old life for a new one that I couldn't even define? I'd had friends, a steady teaching job that was comfortable but other than that, I couldn't see anything happening anymore. It was like each day kept repeating itself. I'd loved Cunningham Falls and now I was wondering what the heck I'd been thinking when I left it for Seaside. I frowned and then tried my best to conjure up a bright smile. "Let's get started!"

I was in it now.

Whether I liked it or not.

And part of me, when that sick part thought of the hot guy who'd just stopped by needing help with gum in what I was assuming was his child's hair, was excited.

If they had men like that here.

What could possibly go wrong?

Chapter Two

Trevor

"DAAADDY!" I winced as Bella held up her arms. She was almost four and had enough bubblegum in her hair to make it look blue instead of blonde. I bit back a curse and held her close in an attempt not to get it caught in my longer hair or, God forbid, an eyelash. "I need you, where you go?"

I was about to answer when Eric laughed. "Gum makes your hair fall out!"

"Daddy!" Bella's eyes filled with unshed tears.

Damnit!

"Eric." I gritted my teeth. "You know that's not true, apologize to your little sister."

He gave her a sloppy grin. "Sorry your hair's going to fall out."

Son of a bitch.

"Eric!" Still holding Bella, I stood, almost knocking over the hot chocolate I'd brought them and the babysitter, who seemed to be more interested in her phone than anything going on in our lavish beach house. "If you can't be nice, I'm going to ground you."

He made a face. "Mom never grounded me."

He was six and a pain in my ass.

"Eric…" I prayed for patience. Hell, I hadn't had patience since my ex-wife decided to run away with a Brazilian boy band member meant for stardom. It had been a year. A year of absolute hell, and now I was one month away from gaining full custody of three kids who looked at me like I was eighty years old and needed help with downloading apps on my cell phone.

How had it come to this?

I winced. I really shouldn't dwell on the how.

She was a beautiful supermodel who wanted "the life."

I gave it to her.

We had kids.

She got bored.

End of story.

Bitch.

I rubbed my chest with my hand. Bella grabbed my fingertips and brought them to her cheek. "You have big hands."

I let out a rough exhale. "Because I'm meant to carry you…all of you, that's what family does."

Eric snorted just as his twin brother made his way down the stairs complaining about his iPad breaking…again.

"Malcom, I'll get to it in a few, all right? I need to talk to your nanny first."

"We don't need a nanny," Malcom said in an authoritative voice.

"Why don't you guys go pick out a movie while we talk?"

Eric grumbled something about being too old for hot chocolate even though he took it and started chugging as he walked up the stairs and Bella followed with her bouncy now short and gum inflicted blonde hair and chipper demeanor.

Which left me.

And Adriana.

"So…" I sat down across from her, folding my hands in front of me, feeling completely out of my element. I was a fucking music producer. I had gold records lining the walls of my house—LA house to be exact, but still. And I'd successfully sold out the last reunion tour with my guys.

And yet there I was.

Stuck.

In Seaside.

Staring at a babysitter who was more interested in her Instagram than letting me know if my kids finished their chores.

"How did they do today?" I leaned back in my chair, going for the casual.

She started typing on her phone like her fingers were on fire.

Mine went off.

I looked down.

Adriana: Good! They played at the park, we made cookies, Eric has an attitude problem, and Malcom asked where babies come from, but Bella colored with me while he pouted. Such cool dudes. Well done old man well done.

I blinked then blinked again. "Did you just…text me your answer?"

Her fingers moved again.

Adriana: Yeaaahhhh?

Me: Speak. With. Your. Voice.

She looked up. "Um, it was a good day. Can I get paid now?"

I rubbed my hands down my face. "Adriana, I pay you to help them, not to just watch them. I want you to engage them, to teach them things. Malcom and Eric start school in a few weeks, Bella's headed off to pre-school." Just the idea of them being away from me for more than a few hours had me feeling panic. "I just, I don't want them to get made fun of for not knowing what a circle is, and I'm trying the best I can but—"

"Are you gonna cry?" She narrowed her eyes. "Because I don't think that's in my job description. And if you want me to teach them like a teacher then you should pay me like a teacher." Her smile was back. God save me from seventeen-year-old girls. "Like with benefits and stuff."

"You know what?" I dug into my back pocket and gave her a crisp hundred dollar bill. "Never mind."

She took the cash. "Oh! I almost forgot, a few friends and I are headed to a music festival tomorrow so I need the week off."

I stared at her, slack-jawed. "Adriana, we've been over this. I'm in the studio all week. I hired you to watch them so I could get this album done." She didn't need to know that I hadn't been able to take the press in Malibu, that going to the grocery store had made all three kids cry when some dick reporter asked if Bella was sad her mommy was gone.

It had been a nightmare.

And then my bandmate and lead singer Will told me that the easiest place to escape was Oregon.

And after visiting last year, I realized he'd had a solid point. Not only did Seaside have three films and a reality show hit based on the town, but some of my closest friends had beach houses there.

Including boy band AD2, the guys said they wanted to raise their kids away from the crazy, which made sense.

It still felt like we'd run away in the middle of the night, leaving a life behind that I didn't even recognize anymore.

"Um." Adrianna waved in front of my face. "You have a stroke or something?"

I made a face. "Seriously? How old do you think I am?"

She gave me a wide-eyed look. "Is this the part where I tell the dad that he's still got it?" She licked her lips and bit down on the bottom one. "Is that why you've been so weird since you hired me? You have a crush on me?"

I refrained from groaning into my hands, barely. "That would be a hard no. I'm an adult, and I'm pretty sure if I asked you to dial 911 you'd send a text instead."

"Hey! Well, you're just some washed-up—"

"I'm going to stop you right there before all of my platinum records fall off the wall and chase you down the street. You're fired."

"What? Because I wouldn't suck your—"

"Wow!" I was seconds away from calling in one of the security guards I'd hired for the kids when I was away during the day. The last thing I needed was a kidnapping. "You can show yourself out."

She rolled her eyes. "Whatever. You couldn't handle me anyway."

That would be because I knew how to handle women, and she was nothing but a girl with an iPhone X and way too much time on her hands.

The door slammed behind her.

And just like that, the crying started.

"Daddy!" Bella wailed. "Eric put more gum in my hair!"

"It's gonna fall out! It's gonna make you bald!" Eric shouted.

"Is it normal for gum to be that sticky?" Malcom asked in a confused voice.

"I don't think that's gum." More from Eric.

"DAD!" Malcom shrieked. "I think it's Gorilla Glue!"

"Son of a bitch!" I roared.

The crying intensified.

Of course I just had to fire the nanny. Fantastic. The album deadline was rearing its ugly head, I had absolutely no help, and my kids were understandably upset that their mom was a selfish bitch.

"Just give me a minute to think," I called up, not that it helped. The crying intensified, something was pushed over, a crash sounded louder, another shriek. A curse word.

"Malcom Jonathan WOOD!" I roared.

"It was Eric!"

"Shit!" Eric repeated over and over again.

My eye twitched as I looked at the fridge and saw the beer waiting inside. Once they were in school it would get better. They'd make friends and—

"Daaaaddy!" Bella ran down the stairs and jumped into my arms. "Eric said it's never going to grow back!"

"Everyone downstairs!" I yelled. "Now!" I kissed Bella on the cheek. "Sweetheart, we'll figure it out. There has to be something at the store we can get that will take it out, all right, maybe we'll try the peanut butter this time?"

"Mom would know," came Malcom's solemn voice as he jumped down the bottom stair. "She always knew what to do when—"

"Yeah well, Mom's not here!" Eric shoved him. "So just drop it."

The pain was evident in Eric's face, in Malcom's voice, hell, in the size of Bella's tears.

I was failing them.

I loved them more than anything in the world.

And I was failing them when they needed me the most.

I let out a helpless sigh. "Coats and shoes, we're going to the store."

Chapter Three

Penelope

I spent the entire day unpacking, downed at least two glasses of wine before crashing on the small couch I'd brought from Montana, and nearly missed my first shift.

I still hadn't showered from the day before, which meant I smelled like potato chips and road kill, but I didn't want to be late, especially since I knew that the alternative was unpacking more boxes and wondering what the heck I was thinking driving from everything I knew in Montana.

To a strange place where I had exactly one friend who barely spent any time in the area because she was married to a famous actor.

Like A-list famous.

What did I expect?

That I'd get here and everything would suddenly feel fresh and perfect just like the salty ocean breeze?

I threw on a Nike sweatshirt, a pair of leggings, tennis shoes, and a Mets baseball hat that I'd purchased on a whim because I liked the colors.

Yeah, I was that person.

I didn't have time to do much to my face, so I swiped it with a makeup wipe, grabbed mascara, and then added a touch of pink lip gloss.

This, I sighed as I stared in the small mirror, was as good as it was going to get.

I exhaled and locked up the house, then made my way over to the small coffee shop. The lights were already on, even though the door was locked. Jennifer said she'd arrive early and get the first pot of coffee going for me so I would actually make it through the busy morning.

I wondered what she meant by busy.

Especially after looking up and down the dead streets of Seaside.

It was five a.m.

And the only things I saw wandering around were seagulls that seemed hell-bent on diving toward the water in search of food.

Despite the tattered screen, the small coffee shop was inviting, homey in a way that made my chest ache.

One thing that the universe never seems to remind you about fresh starts: they're almost always extremely lonely and uncomfortable no matter how fresh they can be.

I loved the ocean.

I loved to travel.

It was an adventure, right?

An adventure at 27.

Don't focus on the past, focus on the now.

The now is all you can control, right? Inhale, exhale, exist in the moment, and make yourself a coffee.

I pulled three espresso shots, dumped them into a cup, added a bit of cream, and chugged the thing before making sure the cash register was flipped on and counting the till.

By the time I was done making sure the store was ready to go, it was time to flip the sign.

How very exciting.

Not.

I flipped from *Closed* to *Open* and took the few steps back behind the counter, wondering if I would need another three shots of coffee. The bell over the door rang.

An elderly man in his seventies gave me a wave with a newspaper. "Extra hot drip, black." He held out exactly one dollar and seventy-five cents and then honest to God dropped a dime in my tip jar.

The only reason I didn't gawk was because he had a Vietnam Vet hat on, and he looked like the sort of old man you'd want as your grandfather, especially during Christmas time—yeah, he'd be the grandpa that would put an orange in everyone's stocking and do magic tricks on your birthday with napkins and pieces of licorice.

Where the heck was I getting all of this?

I needed to stop watching the Hallmark movie channel ASAP.

"Oh!" He turned on his heel and then pointed the same newspaper at me. "Now if we get too loud, just say the word. We can get pretty rowdy!"

I bit back a smile. "I promise I'll let you know. I'm Penelope, by the way."

He beamed. "I know! Jennifer told us all about you. Don't you worry, this is one of the best places to live in the Pacific Northwest. Remember what I said."

"Scout's honor." I winked just as the bell went off again.

Eight more men walked in, all around the same age, with a flurry of canes and walkers, and every single one of them ordered a black coffee except for the last one, who had the most beautiful brown skin and wide smile. "I need a little sugar."

I let out a little laugh. "All right, so you want sugar in your coffee?"

"Oh no, I think I want a latte today, can you surprise me?"

"You mean with the flavor?"

He gave me a sheepish grin. "Every day's a new day, isn't it? Why not try something new? Life's too short, Penelope."

Did everyone know my name?

"Okay." I quickly pulled his shot, steamed the milk and handed him his drink.

Exact change.

Again.

Well, at least my job was easy.

The morning crowd was indeed loud, but only because they were arguing about football. Apparently, we had a few Seahawks fans still upset over the Patriots beating them in the Super Bowl.

It was hard not to grin as they bickered.

"....they're a running team and they threw the damn ball!"

"I knew it was PI the minute it happened."

"Lucky catch."

Smiling, I cleaned out the machine just as a few high school girls walked in with their backpacks secured on their backs and an astonishing amount of makeup painted across their young faces. "What can I get you girls?"

I didn't have to guess. They would want frappuccinos. I would bet my life on it.

"Two frappuccinos." The first girl gave me a weird look and then handed me a twenty. "With extra whip."

"What size?"

"Sixteen." She stared down at her phone. "Anyways, you were saying?"

"He fired me!" the other girl complained. "And he made fun of me, and then he thought I called him old. Whatever, I don't even know, it was so strange. At first I thought he was hitting on me then he looked so offended that I don't know, adults are weird and his kids were so annoying!"

"But he paid you like a hundred bucks for three hours," the friend pointed out. "I'd put up with a lot for that kind of money, even if it meant babysitting some famous guy's kids."

"He's not that famous." She sniffed.

Still eavesdropping, I got them their change and grabbed their cups.

"Adrenaline won two Grammys last year, one for song of the year." My ears perked. Adrenaline? The Adrenaline? Hottest boy band from my teen years? I had posters of them in my room when I was fifteen and was convinced I was going to marry the lead singer.

And then I went to a concert and the drummer caught my eye.

Golden brown hair, sexy eyes, and…

Wait.

Why did that seem familiar?

Huh. I made their drinks, the noise from the blender shutting out any more of my eavesdropping, sadly. Did that mean that Adrenaline was here? In this town? Wouldn't Dani have told me? According to her, a lot of the celebs refused to spend the winter in Seaside since it got so cold. They all ran back to LA, only to return to Seaside during the summer.

Not that it mattered.

"Here you go." I handed the girls their drinks.

"I said extra whipped cream." The one grumpy girl who had been fired turned her nose up at me. Perfect. Insulted by a girl who was going to be buried with her phone actually grown into her palm from usage.

"Sorry." I pulled the lids off, added more whip cream, and handed them back.

"You must be new." The girl's eyes narrowed.

"Yup." I had so many other things I wanted to say, but I refrained when the bell dinged again, and this time a hushed silence filled the room.

"That's him," Rude Girl said under her breath, her cheeks reddening.

Her friend's eyes widened in shock like she wasn't sure if she should pass out or say hi.

"Trevor!" One of the old guys stood and patted him on the back. "How's the album coming?"

Trevor, Trevor, Trevor. Holy.

Stay calm.

Calm.

Trevor Wood.

And he'd been in here the day before.

What was he doing here? Wasn't he married?

With kids?

Living happily ever after?

The girls scooted out of the coffee shop so fast it looked like their little trendy backpacks were on fire.

And then a chubby little face peered over the counter at me. "I like hot chocolate."

The poor thing had just gotten a haircut, and from the looks of it, her hairdresser had either been drunk or...

"Got all the gum out?" I leaned down so we were both at eye level across the counter.

Her eyes looked puffy from tears. "Yeah, Daddy said it will grow back."

"It will," I soothed. "I cut my bangs to here when I was about your age." I pointed to the top of my forehead. "And my hair grew back just fine."

"You have pretty hair." Her teeth looked like little Chiclets. Be still my heart, she was freaking adorable. And she said I had pretty hair even though I hadn't washed it in five days and smelled like car.

"Thank you." I beamed. "So why don't I grab you some hot chocolate? With sprinkles?"

"Red ones!" She clapped her hands. "Please?"

"Coming right up." A shadow descended over me. I was still at eye level, so I had to look up, up, up, up directly into Trevor Wood's penetrating and amused stare. "Hey there."

My voice croaked.

I smelled.

And I was hunched down nearly touching the floor.

I quickly stood and nearly collided with the old cash register before tugging my black apron down and focusing in on his smirk. "I see you fixed the hair?"

He frowned and then gave his head a shake. "Right, yeah, well, I'm not so sure we're calling it fixed, but it's better and both brothers have been grounded for using Gorilla Glue after spending hours getting the gum out."

I gasped. "Gorilla Glue?"

"It's been an exciting twenty-four hours," he said in a tired voice. "I told them I'd buy each of them a pony if we could stop and get coffee."

"And when you don't follow through?" I crossed my arms.

"I didn't specify what kind of pony. They have them at the dollar store, about this big." He held up his fingers an inch apart. "Brown. Three for one dollar."

"Trickery." I nodded.

"Warfare," he deadpanned just as one of the boys behind him kicked the other in the shin.

"Take it back, Eric! Take it back!"

"It's true! Mom left because of you!"

My heart cracked while Trevor flipped around and grabbed Eric by the shoulders. "Son, we don't say things like that."

"Who cares?!" Tears filled his eyes. "It doesn't even matter anymore."

The shop went quiet.

Even the old timers were staring.

Eric clutched his dad's hands. "Maybe if we weren't born..."

Oh, my heart.

The little girl gasped, her lower lip wobbling.

"Hey." I tried distracting her. "Wanna help make the hot chocolate?"

"Could I?" Her eyes were so big, so innocent. What sort of person left this messy perfection?

"Of course!"

The little boy closest to us looked between his dad's hushed conversation with Eric and the girl as she made her way around the register.

"You can help too," I offered.

He took one look at his dad then me, and suddenly he and the girl were by my side while I grabbed them each a cup and showed them how to pump the chocolate.

"What are your names?" I asked casually.

"Bella." The girl licked some chocolate off of her finger after dipping it in the cup.

"Malcom." The boy's voice was soft, almost like he was afraid to talk too loud, or maybe just taught not to talk to strangers.

"Those are some pretty awesome names." I steamed the milk. "All right, guys, so each of you get a spoon so you can stir really hard when I pour the milk in, and remember it's hot so we have to be really careful."

"Okay!" they said in unison. I handed each of them a spoon and poured the milk in. Bella's sloshed a bit, but Malcom was determined as he focused on the spoon, stirring all the chocolate in.

While they were busy, I made the same coffee I'd made the day previous for Trevor and another hot chocolate for the other little boy.

"All finished?" I asked once Bella took a sip.

"Mmm." Milk had found its way onto her upper lip. "So good!"

"It's better when you work for it yourself, right?" I ran a hand through her short hair and frowned. It was actually longer than it looked, and we didn't have any more customers coming through the doors. "Want me to braid it?"

"My mom used to braid it," she said into her cup and then looked up after drinking several more gulps. "Braids are my favorite."

"All right then." I grabbed a rubber band from my wrist and quickly tugged the larger pieces back into a braid and tied everything together while Malcom finished his hot chocolate and started pumping more chocolate into his cup.

Boys.

By the time we were done, I realized we'd been hanging out for at least ten minutes. Where was...?

I looked up.

Trevor stared at me with stars in his eyes, actual stars. Or maybe it was me, maybe I was the one with stars in my eyes.

"You're hired," was what came out.

"Huh?" I tilted my head. "For?"

"Dad fired our nanny." The boy next to him crossed his arms. "She was on her phone a lot."

I surpassed a laugh. "Oh?"

"She was so annoying," he continued. "And she always asked about Dad. It was weird."

I made a face.

Trevor just shook his head as if to say leave it.

"I'm sorry," I found myself saying. "I have a job, I actually just started yesterday and—"

"What are your hours?" He took a step closer. I had no escape. I could see the flecks of gold in his green eyes, could almost taste his cologne. The guy was built for being so tall. He was at least six four and had enough muscle that it was noticeable through his white Henley.

Tattoos swirled and peeked out from under the collar running halfway up his neck, and he had both ears pierced.

Yeah, he looked nothing like a dad.

More like his tour bus forgot him in Seaside.

Did he live here on purpose?

"Um, my hours." I found my voice. "I work until noon Monday through Friday and on the weekends I work all day Saturday."

"Could you do one to seven every afternoon? Weekends off? I'd pay well."

"Um…"

Bella looked up at me with her wide eyes and nodded her head like I should say yes, like it was the best idea ever to take a job with my junior high crush and try not to stare at him all day.

His life.

His family.

His kids.

My fresh start.

Hah, my fresh start did not include becoming a nanny to a rock star.

"Please?" Bella slid her hand into mine and squeezed. "I miss having my hair braided."

That was all it took.

A little girl's sticky hands, milk mustache, and a sad-looking braid, to say yes to a man who I could swear no human had ever said no to in his entire life.

And I knew in that moment. I was completely and utterly screwed.

Chapter Four

Trevor

I woke up the next morning to a pounding headache and Bella sitting on my chest asking for peanut butter pancakes. Something flew into my room. A ball? A spaceship? Who knew at this point?

And then crying.

All the crying.

"He hit me with the ball!" Bella wailed and wrapped her arms around my neck. I just laid there staring up at the ceiling wondering how I was messing it up so horribly. Josie had a lot of faults, but at least she'd been a good stay-at-home mom, until she couldn't handle the fact that I was touring for an entire year, leaving her in the dust.

Her words, not mine.

She left me the night of the Grammys.

I got a Grammy, and she walked out of my life because she was jealous.

I saw it for what it was.

Knew several Hollywood couples who said the very reason they never dated or married someone in the same industry was because you were always competing for roles, fame, Instagram followers.

I held on to Bella until she stopped crying.

"All better?" I asked in my raspy sleep-filled voice. I'd at least gotten five hours last night. I needed to lay some more tracks. Each of the guys had taken a much-needed break and decided to drop a solo album.

Our manager was thrilled.

Our agent was swimming in money.

And since I owned my own studio back in Malibu and now one in Seaside, I'd known it would be easy to do too, except now I wasn't so sure.

What was I supposed to do? Take the kids with me on tour? They'd done a few cities with me last year, but I didn't want to take them out of school.

With a deep breath, I heaved Bella into the air and threw my feet over the side of the bed, landing on a few misplaced Legos that had my eyes watering and curse words screaming inside my head. There was a reason they weren't allowed in my room. Legos.

"Daddy hurt?" Bella cupped my face.

"A bit," I lied. Son of a bitch, I was going to get rid of every last Lego in that house. "Just...give me a minute."

"Your face is red," she pointed out with a grin, damn her and those dimples. "Are you saying crap in your head?"

I had told her crap was a bad word that adults said when they were angry and that if she was really *really* angry, she could use it like her brothers.

Yes, the answer is yes; it has backfired one hundred percent.

"Boys!" I called downstairs while Malcom and Eric chased each other around the island in the kitchen. "Get the pancake mix out!"

They grumbled.

More things were thrown.

Chaos. I lived in absolute chaos.

Exhausted, even though my day was just starting, I carried Bella down the stairs and started in on the pancakes, all the while staring at the clock with relief. Five hours. In five hours, the new nanny would be here.

Fingers crossed the twins didn't set her on fire.

And maybe she'd braid Bella's hair again.

My gut clenched.

I'd felt like a complete idiot staring at the pretty barista with my jaw hanging to the floor. She'd wrangled in my kids faster than I did. They reacted to her in a way I hadn't seen in a really long time.

It had been such a relief that for a minute all I could do was stare.

She had flawless, makeup-free skin, and her hair was in this adorable ponytail poking out of a Met's hat. I couldn't tell if she was in her early twenties or late. Maybe all the Botox I'd been exposed to in LA was messing with my head. I hated guessing ages because I was almost always wrong. Look at the ex.

"Dad?" Eric interrupted my thoughts.

"Yeah, buddy?" I snapped out of it and grabbed a mixing bowl.

"You're smiling awful big over pancakes."

Little shit. I stared him down and winked. "That's because I'm adding chocolate chips!"

"Hooray!" Bella squealed in delight while Malcom and Eric gave each other high fives then grabbed their iPads and sat at the breakfast bar.

Coffee.

Would it be wrong to train my children how to make me coffee so that I at least had a cup waiting when I woke up to multiple screams, tears, and flying objects?

I heaved a sigh. It would probably have seven Legos and a booger.

At this point, I would take it all and say God bless you every one.

I grabbed a pod for the Keurig, yawned, and made myself a cup while Bella tried mixing the batter. She had more outside the bowl than inside, but she liked to stir.

She started helping cook when she was two.

And couldn't say stir to save her life, which only meant I stared at her like an idiot until she grabbed a spoon. "Sway sway sway!"

That was her word for stir.

It was a conundrum.

At least she was helpful while her brothers literally watched other children play with toys on YouTube.

Something was very wrong with people in this world if that was a thing. I watched one episode of a guy singing Best Friend Best Friend while opening candy and nearly called the police.

Because if that doesn't scream pedophile, than I really don't know what does.

Coffee brewed, and pan on, I grabbed the bowl from Bella and started to pour out the pancakes.

I felt slightly guilty when I eyed the clock again.

My fingers twitched with the need to play out my frustration on the drums, with the need to write music and send it to the guys to see if it was good enough. And on top of that, I had band AD2 coming in at the end of the week to lay two tracks.

Technically, they lived here only during the summer months, but now that Alec, the older brother, had a kid with another one on the way, they were thinking about staying permanently because of schools.

My plate was full.

And I was ready to offer the new nanny a million dollars plus benefits if she'd just clean up the Legos.

That was when you knew you were at your limit—when you would pay a complete stranger to pick up the hazardous toys sprinkled around your house like miniature bombs ready to go off.

"ERIC!" Malcom screamed. "STOP TOUCHING ME!"

I chugged my coffee, burning my tongue in the process, and eyed the clock again. Five hours, I could last five hours. Right?

Chapter Five

Penelope

All I had was a phone number to text and an address.

He said I'd have to sign something once I reported to work. I assumed it was something legal that basically said I wouldn't go to TMZ and tell them what kind of body wash he used.

What sort of person did that anyways?

And why would something like that even matter?

I pushed the doorbell.

Heard screaming.

Almost backed away when the screaming intensified and smiled when I heard heavy footsteps and then, "This is your last warning before a time out!"

The door opened.

Trevor had ketchup all over his deep V-neck T-shirt, some sort of food object stuck to his skinny jeans, and he was wearing one purple sock.

Nothing out of the ordinary per se.

Except he had a pink boa on and a tiara.

"Wow, had I known I was meeting royalty today, I would have dressed up," I teased, shocking even myself. We didn't know each other enough to tease, but he seemed relieved as he exhaled and then burst out laughing.

"Tea time." He nodded. "All the Brits do it."

"Ah, I see. Do you use an accent and everything?"

"I attempted one time, and my daughter cried because she thought I was making fun of hers, so no, I use my boring dad voice." He winked.

Yeah, nothing about him was boring even covered in ketchup and mystery food, and he was still one of the best looking men I'd ever seen up close.

Period.

He could take a shower under a sewer, and women would still crane their necks to get a better look at him.

It was alarming.

And honestly, I needed to get a grip before my inner fangirl let loose an ear piercing scream that would match the rest of the noise coming from upstairs.

"Thank you so much." Trevor took off his tiara. "For starting so soon. I'm swamped and since their mom left—" He cut himself off, but something indefinable flickered in his eyes. "It's just...been a big adjustment for us."

My chest cracked a bit. "Has she been gone long?"

"Gone," he repeated and then smiled. "Gone makes it sound like she's missing or that maybe she didn't choose to leave. She's called twice in the past year since she left, sends the kids presents on all their birthdays, and for the holidays flew in for twenty-four hours before jet setting back to Brazil or wherever the hell her current boy toy is. She left. And I don't think I'll ever forgive her for doing that to our family."

"I'm so sorry," I blurted, feeling horrible. "It's none of my business. I feel horrible, I'm—"

"Honestly, I thought you probably knew. The rest of the world does." His eyes locked onto mine.

"Well, here's a moment of truth—I don't read celebrity gossip and have been living in Montana for the last few years of my life, where the local gossip is even dirtier than Hollywood."

"Oh?" He crossed his bulky arms.

"Yeah, I mean we once had this horse escape..." I grinned and bit down on my bottom lip, trying like hell not to look at the complete package of perfection in front of me as he waited for me to continue. "Since you were honest, I guess it's my turn. I came here for a fresh start. My cousin Dani's married to Lincoln Greene."

"Ahhhhhhh." Trevor snapped his fingers. "I love Lincoln, he's one of the good ones."

"He's the best, they both are. It was their idea, and here I am."

"Huh." Trevor seemed to mull that over a bit before another yell came from upstairs. A basketball was thrown over the railing; it bounced behind him while he looked up and bit back a curse. "I apologize in advance. Just remember, I'm paying you well."

"I love kids so it won't be a problem." What was I saying? I loved kids, yes, but not ones who were hurting and who lashed out and yelled and cried, and crap I was in over my head, totally in over my head. Back when I was a teacher we had school counselors for this sort of thing, I knew how to teach them things, to engage, but the sadness factor or even the anger, I wasn't so sure about.

"Well, just in case…" He grabbed a piece of paper from the kitchen table. "You have my personal cell number, and if you sign here we'll be in business."

"NDA?" I guessed.

He gave me a funny look. "Well, yeah, but it's more or less a contract in writing that states you won't sell pictures of my kids on the internet."

I gaped. "People do that?"

"You'd be surprised what people would do for money," was all he said as he handed me a pen.

I scribbled my name across the dotted line and handed the pen back to him, his fingers warm as they grazed my skin.

I felt that touch more than a nanny should.

This was going to be a problem.

The awareness I had of him.

The way I couldn't stop looking at him.

And the way he seemed to be doing the same to me.

"So." I rocked back on my heels. "I'm going to assume by the ketchup on your shirt that they've had lunch and that now we're doing play time. Do they take naps?"

"They have quiet time at three, and a lot of times all three of them crash."

"Great!" A sleeping kid was a healthy kid. And it would give me time to clean up the train wreck that had exploded around his house. "And you'll be home at?"

"Six." He blinked his gorgeous eyes at me. "Thank you for this. I don't know what else to say."

"No problem." I grinned. "Maybe change your shirt before heading out, though? We don't want people thinking you murdered someone just because they see a flash of red ketchup."

"Good point." He laughed and peeled the shirt over his head with record finesse and speed.

I shivered, gaped, and then didn't know if I was supposed to be outraged or turn away.

I turned away.

"Damn it. Sorry, it's just been us, I wasn't thinking, plus the laundry is on the couch—"

"Don't worry about it." I felt my face flame as visions of his six pack taunted my mind. "I'll make sure to fold it when you're gone."

"Great." In a flurry of movements, he had a black band shirt on and was calling upstairs. "Kids, I'm going to the studio, Penelope's here to hang out with you. Don't burn the house down and listen to her, all right?"

Silence.

"KIDS!"

"Okay, Dad."

"Sure."

"You hid the matches!"

Trevor gave me a panicked look.

"We'll be fine." Matches? Burning the house down? What kind of kids burned the house down at age five? Or even thought that attempting it would be a solid life choice? I gave what I hoped was a reassuring smile, or even a non-reassuring one. "Promise!"

"You're sure." He eyed me like he wasn't above chasing me out the door and pinning me to the ground just to make sure I'd stay.

"Yeah." I waved him off. "Go before they catch the scent of freedom."

He barked out a laugh. "You're not wrong."

"Dad!"

I gave him a wide-eyed look while he nearly tripped over a Lego and made a run for it out the front door.

I felt three sets of eyes watching my back.

Slowly I turned and crossed my arms. "Who wants to make a fort?"

Every set of eyes lit up.

Hours later, while the kids all crashed in their rooms, I realized I'd grossly misjudged my ability to be a good nanny.

They wanted me to play with them the entire time, which I loved, but it also meant breaking up a fight every few minutes over stupid things like skin touching skin, being scared of a monster face that one of the twins kept doing, and my personal favorite.

The book.

That was all Bella said. The book was angry.

And then she said her doll laughed at her under her bed.

I was pretty sure that any sort of paranormal Annabelle activity wasn't part of the job description, but Malcom finally fessed up to pretending to be her doll.

All in all, it was a busy day.

I'd cleaned the entire kitchen, tossed out old takeout, and noticed that the freezer had a perfectly good beef roast in it.

I defrosted it and added it to a pan with some carrots, potatoes, onions, and some spices. It wasn't gourmet, but at least the kids would have a nice home-cooked meal, right along with Trevor.

I started in on the laundry at around a quarter till five, after checking on the kids again and finding they were still out.

There was enough laundry on that couch waiting to get folded I was shocked that everyone wasn't roaming the house naked.

I winced. Bad visual.

You're the nanny.

I picked up something black.

Black boxer briefs.

Not toddler size.

Big boy size.

Had anyone told me a few months ago that my fresh start would include folding Trevor Wood's underwear, I would have checked them for a head injury.

And yet there I was, clutching his boxer briefs to my chest like a stalker fan gone too far.

I folded and folded and folded until I heard the sleepy talk coming from upstairs as each kid made their way down to the main living room. I already had apples and juice boxes out for everyone and a Blippi streaming via Amazon.

Everyone just huddled on the main couch with their snacks while I finished folding.

Malcom yawned and struggled with the straw to his juice box while Bella grabbed what looked like a black T-shirt and tried wrapping it around her legs. It wasn't fitting right, so I walked over to help when Eric's tiny hand shot out and shoved me away.

I wasn't sure what to do.

He didn't exactly hit me but he did shove me.

I squinted down at him. He just shook his head and mouthed the word *"Don't."*

"Why?" I whispered back.

He looked down, not before I saw anger flashing across his features, and then he was on his feet and stomping back up the stairs.

Malcom let out a little sigh and then cupped his mouth with both hands. "That was one of Mom's shirts, she can't leave the house without it."

My heartbeat stuttered, and then pain sliced through my chest as I tried to imagine knowing my mom left me by choice, at such a young age.

"Malcom? Why don't we go into the kitchen real quick?"

Bella was enraptured with both the black T-shirt and the TV show. Obviously, she was still trying to wake up.

Malcom obediently followed me into the kitchen. I leaned down to his level. "Does she get upset if anyone touches the shirt?"

He nodded and then his lower lip started to wobble.

I was not prepared for this.

Not at all.

I reached for him just as he burst into tears.

Oh, God.

I didn't know the woman, and I wanted to strangle her with my bare hands then run her over with my Jeep.

"It's okay." I hugged him close.

His tiny arms tried to fit around me, and then he stepped back and wiped his face.

"I'm not supposed to cry in front of Bella," he said between sobs. "But I miss Mom. She left us, and she did it on purpose."

I squeezed my eyes shut and prayed for some sort of wisdom to give the kid, but I had nothing, because I couldn't imagine it, couldn't justify it one bit. I'd always wanted kids and that old resentment came flaring to life at the thought of someone being blessed with three and walking away.

I'd already been told it would be hard to get pregnant.

She'd had everything.

Everything I'd always wanted.

How did a person just...leave?

"I'm so sorry." I wiped the tears on his soft, puffy cheeks as he stared down at his feet. "When I get sad about things, sometimes I think about the things I should be happy about."

"Yeah?" He swiped his nose with his sleeve. "Like what?"

"Well..." I smiled wide. "You have a pretty cool dad. I mean, who can say their dad is an actual rock star?"

He shrugged a shoulder. "I like firefighters."

I almost burst out laughing. "Well, I think that rock stars are cooler than firefighters. I bet most of the world knows who your dad is, plus he makes people happy with his music. How cool is that?"

He frowned and then squinted at me. "I like his music."

"I bet that's a relief for your dad."

Malcom grinned. "I still wish my mom was here."

"That's okay, little man. I promise one day it won't make you as sad, and for what it's worth I think you're pretty awesome."

He grinned, put his arms around me again, and then paled. "You aren't leaving, are you?"

That was it, I was officially stealing Trevor's kid. He'd be fine, he had two more. Right? A smile tugged at my lips. "Only to go home and sleep in my own bed."

"You can sleep here!" Malcom grinned and then clapped his hands. "Dad has lots of rooms. I know sometimes he has friends over that are girls, but they don't stay long."

"Ummm." I felt myself blushing. "Well, I'm staying longer. That's why I'm going back to my house, because all my things are there."

"Oh." He frowned. "I guess that makes sense."

"Yup! Now, why don't you go back and sit with your sister while I check on dinner, okay?"

"'K!" He ran off, his little legs sprinting him into the next room while I turned around and nearly had a frigging heart attack.

"Trevor!" I stumbled back, colliding with the granite countertop. "How long have you been standing there?"

His face was unreadable. I wracked my brain trying to think of what I could have said that was wrong and came up empty.

"You." He shook his head. "He hugged you."

"Is that…" Oh no! He didn't want me touching his kids! "I'm so sorry. I didn't know that was a rule. I swear I won't hug him. He was just crying and he was—"

"He hasn't hugged anyone but me since his mom left, and even then I have to basically beg him." Sadness flashed across his face. "Thank you…for what you said, for taking the time to listen to him, to get down on his level. My kids are…everything."

"I know," I said softly. "I didn't want to poison the well either, with their mom. As far as I'm concerned, that won't help anything, so I hope that what I said was okay?"

"Agreed." He sighed like he'd spent the last few hours under extreme stress, and then he perked up and sniffed the air. "Pot roast?"

I beamed. "Yeah, I figured you'd be starving and the kids slept late, probably because we played so hard, which also means that's my cue to leave. I had a long day in the play room upstairs. It won by the way."

He burst out laughing. "Yeah, it often does. It's the Legos."

"Totally." I smiled back at him as we fell into silence. "All right then." I took a step backwards. "The laundry's folded, dinner's ready, and—"

"Stay." He took a step toward me.

What was happening?

"Um, no, really it's fine. I don't want to intrude."

"It's the least I can do." His sexy smile was back. Ugh, pair that with the fact that he had three of the most adorable kids, not to mention that he used to be a poster on my wall. Torture. You grow up looking at boy bands and celebrities and dreaming about meeting them backstage and marrying them later and then you laugh with your friends.

And then the next day, you're folding their underwear and making a pot roast.

Huh.

"Please stay!" Bella came stumbling into the kitchen, the black T-shirt still clutched in her right hand, her monkey in the other.

Trevor's smile fell. "Hey, baby girl, you have a good nap?"

She nodded and then lifted the shirt to his face. "It doesn't smell like her anymore."

"I'll take care of it." He kissed her forehead. "Why don't you run off and get your brothers while we get dinner ready?"

"Yay! She's staying!" She did a little twirl and then whispered in a loud voice. "I like Penny."

He frowned. "Penny?"

"Penelope was a mouthful," I added with a smile of my own.

"Gotcha." He winked at me, making my heart flutter and my stomach drop to my knees. The guy needed to be careful who he winked at. I knew I was blushing. I told my body to stop betraying me, but my face just got hotter. Perfect.

I quickly turned around and made myself busy grabbing plates.

Just focus on setting the table.

Not the image of his abs burned into your brain.

Or his wink.

Or the way he wore a shirt.

Lord, have mercy on us mere mortals.

Amen.

Chapter Six

Trevor

The last time we all sat down as a family for dinner was when my wife was still around.

Though she always hated staying in.

I couldn't even remember how many times she called a sitter without asking me so that we could go to the latest party or premiere. I was sick of it but hated the fight that followed if I wanted to stay home.

"Why don't you cook like this?" Eric asked, shoving another piece of pot roast smothered in ketchup into his mouth and chewing like he hadn't had real food in months. Little shit. "Is this what home-cooked meals taste like?"

I narrowed my eyes then tossed my napkin in his direction. It didn't make it very far, which just made the rest of the kids laugh and point.

God, I loved them.

"I'm glad you guys like it." Penelope beamed and then dipped her napkin in her water and dabbed the ketchup from Bella's face.

She was so natural with them.

Every sitter we'd ever had had been older, mainly because Josephine was paranoid that someday I'd end up sleeping with the nanny. Not that she had any reason not to trust me. She was the cheater. I was the one who was in it for the long term.

I shook my head, trying to get my thoughts away from my failed marriage and on being present for my kids.

On my music.

Penelope squeezed Bella's hand.

I gripped my fork so hard I half expected it to bend in my palm. Bella deserved that, all three of them deserved that.

Someone to make them pot roast.

Someone to wipe their faces.

They had me, but I wanted them to have more. They deserved to have everything, and I didn't know how to do that, at least not while I was still figuring out what it meant to be a single dad with three kids under the age of seven.

"Did you guys have fun today?" I asked, standing and picking up dishes to go wash in the sink.

"Yes!" Bella shouted first. "And we had juice!"

"Best day ever," I teased while Eric gave a little eye roll and shrugged. At least he was eating. He didn't have much of an appetite, and I knew it was because he missed his mom.

Anger was his way of dealing with things.

He was so like me, it was painful to watch.

I had always had music to ground me, though, music to escape. Eric had no interest in music. He loved video games, which meant I basically had no even playing ground since I hated anything to do with social media and TV. I gave them a little screen time during the day, but I wanted them to be kids, to run outside, play, get dirty, build a treehouse.

Supervised, but still.

"You seem lost in your thoughts," Penelope whispered as she joined me by the sink and started drying the plates as I handed them to her. "Did everything go okay at the studio?"

I almost dropped the plate. "Wow, first pot roast, now you're asking about my day?"

I didn't mean to sound like a jackass, but that was exactly how it came out.

She squeezed her eyes shut like she was in pain and took a deep breath. "Sorry, that's not...you know what, I should go." With shaky hands, she set the plate down. Her smile was forced as she said goodbye to the kids and promised to see them the next day.

And I stood at the sink like a dick for another ten minutes before grabbing a few board games for the kids and setting them up at the kitchen table with ice cream.

Once they were all settled with Guess Who, I grabbed my phone and walked into the living room.

Me: I'm sorry. That came out wrong.

I could tell she was typing.

Why the hell was I sweating?

Maybe because she was beautiful, and I'd been ignoring that fact for the last twenty-four hours even while I was caught staring at her during dinner.

Maybe because I'd lashed out.

I groaned and ran a hand through my messy hair.

Penelope: That's okay. I don't want you to think I'm intruding on your family in any way. Boundaries are good. I'll be more professional, I promise.

Shit.

I didn't want professional.

I wanted...

If the guys could see me now.

I wanted a damn adult friend.

I wanted someone I could talk to about my kids.

I was...lonely.

Funny how you can be surrounded by fame, fortune, people shouting your name, and you still feel like the most isolated person on the planet.

Me: God no, please don't. If one more person smiles at me and tells me it's going to be okay I'm going to lose my mind. I need more adult friends who aren't happy bandmates or people who want something from me. Sorry, overshare.

Penelope: That's not an overshare. And I get you. I just moved here, remember?

Me: Is this the point in the conversation that I ask if we can maybe hang out? As adults sometime? Not a date.

Great, I really was going to die alone with my drumsticks clutched in my hand. Music would be my mistress. Fantastic. The guys always did tease me about music being more important than anything.

But they didn't know. It was the only thing that never let me down. It was my constant. I needed it like I needed air to survive.

Penelope: Hah don't worry I'm a good adult friend. I'm an even better friend because I won't hit on you. I don't date famous people. I don't want anything to do with the spotlight. I've seen what Dani goes through. I mean, not that you'd be interested. That came out wrong. My turn to apologize…

I grinned down at my phone.

Me: You mean you didn't have a poster of me in your bedroom when you were fourteen? I'm almost insulted.

Penelope: I may never show my face again. Guilty. One poster, but I was more of an Andrew girl.

Me: You're fired.

Penelope: But the drummer and sometimes lead vocalist did have a really great…

I could have sworn I started to sweat. What was I? A teenager again? Not that I'd even dated much, I was too petrified I'd somehow knock up a groupie or end up in the tabloids.

Me: Great?

Penelope: Beat ;) He had a great beat, nice hair too, teeth—

Me: Are you trying to bruise my ego?

Penelope: Is it working?

Me: No, not really. I saw you staring at my abs today.

Penelope: OMG who just changes in front of strangers! You deserved that! I didn't know where to look, okay?

I burst out laughing.

"Dad? Someone here?" Eric called.

"No, no, sorry just, something funny….on Facebook," I lied.

"Can you come help us? Bella wants to keep playing, but she keeps guessing wrong on purpose."

"Do not!" Bella yelled.

"Do too!" the boys said in unison.

I sighed.

Apparently I was done texting a beautiful woman.

Shit.

A beautiful woman who was watching my kids.

Who I had no business involving myself with.

Who had just agreed to be my platonic friend.

I quickly typed out a message so she wouldn't think I'd left her hanging.

Me: Kids are calling and sorry about changing in front of you. Next time I'll ask permission. Not that there will be a next time. I think I need a re-do of this conversation. See you tomorrow, Penny.

I didn't realize until I was lying in bed that night, with Bella and her black T-shirt on my right and Malcom on my left with his purple teddy and Eric with his mouth open snoring..

We'd already given her a nickname.

And it had only been two days.

A handful of hours.

And for some stupid reason I refused to rationalize, I fell asleep with a smile on my face.

Chapter Seven

Penelope

The next day at the coffee shop, I found myself checking my phone like someone obsessed.

It wasn't even that I was expecting him to text me.

It was one hundred percent that I wanted him to.

That I liked talking with him.

And that was a problem.

I decided to text my best friend Fallon from back home. Maybe she'd at least have some stellar advice even if the advice was for me to stop acting like a teenager waiting for a phone call.

Me: So I may be working for someone famous, not the plan, remember the band Adrenaline?

Fallon wasted no time.

Fallon: TELL ME EVERYTHING, and I thought you were working at a coffee shop. In fact you sent me a picture of you at that very coffee shop yesterday morning? Did you quit? Why aren't you keeping me updated? Also if you don't respond asap you're dead.

Ugh I missed her so much.

Me: I may be working for Trevor Wood as a part time nanny before his kids start school and I may have said yes without thinking and now I'm staring at my phone like I'm more than the hired help and I'm one day in.

Fallon: Trevor Wood. The Trevor Wood? Hottest drummer alive?

Six pack for days? That Trevor Wood?

Me: Yes, focus! We texted a bit last night and, he was flirty, I was flirty...

Fallon: Aw, did he pass you a note in biology too? Maybe you guys can play MASH later!

I rolled my eyes and smiled down at the house, car, and vacation emoji.

Me: Very funny. I need you to virtually slap me so I stop overthinking this. I'm the nanny. That's it.

Fallon: Consider yourself slapped, you're the nanny but that doesn't mean you can't still be open to something more...adventurous. I mean that is why you abandoned us, isn't it? You needed a change of scenery and God in his mysterious ways gave you Trevor Wood! Bitch.

I laughed out loud.

Me: So...just roll with it?

Fallon: I want notes at the end of every day. Or I'm killing you.

Me: I miss you.

Fallon: I miss you too. Facetime later?

Me: Yes please.

Fallon: Preferably when you're at work, I wouldn't be mad.

Me: Signed an NDA so not a word!

Fallon: My lips are sealed. Love you.

Me: You too.

I set my phone down and sighed. This was ridiculous. And I knew better than to even be tempted by him.

After all, famous people were a big *no* in my family. I saw what Dani had to sacrifice just to have a normal life, and all I'd ever really wanted was an adventure, to settle down, not suddenly crush on a rock star and his three kids.

If only he wasn't so sexy.

Or good with his kids.

His hands.

Ugh, I was torturing myself, wasn't I? I'd even started playing the band's last album while I got ready that morning. I almost tripped and face planted against the toilet when one of the songs came on that he sang.

His voice was like velvet and rasp all mixed up with perfect pitch.

Not that I was an expert, but I'd always loved the way he sang, as if all that mattered was him and the song, nothing else.

Jennifer had left a note that she was going to be out running errands, and the day had started off pretty busy, which again was surprising for a small town like Seaside.

I had about an hour before I needed to be at Trevor's house when the bell chimed.

"Be right with—" I gawked. "DANI!"

"HEY!" She rushed toward me. Lincoln, her husband, stood behind her with a giant grin on his face. The guy had a hat on and sunglasses, but any idiot could tell it was Lincoln Greene, A-list actor. He was too good looking to go unnoticed, and people knew he had a beach house here along with every other friggin' celebrity, it seemed.

"I thought you guys were staying in LA for a while." I loved Dani so much, she was just good, one of those people you want to be around, like she couldn't help but be the kindest person you've ever met.

"About that." She bit down on her lower lip and then burst out, "I'm pregnant!"

"WHAT?!" I shrieked. "That's amazing!"

She was young, like really young in my mind. She and Lincoln had fallen for each other a little over a year ago, and at eighteen, she had decided that he was it, and they were going to get married.

The rest was history.

But when you know, you know.

"I know!" She winked back at Lincoln. "It wasn't really in the plan yet, but I'm super excited. We wanted to lay low and celebrate where we first met, so we invited the gang to hang out for the next two weeks starting with an insane barbecue tonight! Can you make it?"

"Um…" Did I tell her about the new job? Technically, I got off in time to actually go, right? "Yeah, that should work."

"Your eyes are shifty." She leaned in. "And you look guilty, like when you got caught behind the bleachers after homecoming."

"Okay, first off, you're the little snitch that was visiting and told my parents I was making out with Pete." I glared. "And second, aren't I older than you?"

"Semantics." Dani's eyes narrowed. "Did you meet someone?"

"In Seaside?" I countered, crossing my arms.

"Please, it's like the best place to meet someone. Linc didn't even stand a chance."

"It's amazing how much she talks now, all things considered," he teased with a wink in my direction. After her parents died, Dani had become a selective mute. Nobody knew how or why, and it had taken Linc to pull her out of it. He smiled at me again. Damn, she needed to keep the guy on a leash. He was almost as sexy as Trevor.

And there it was.

"What was that?" Dani pointed at my face. "You're thinking of someone."

"Huh?" I touched my cheeks with both hands. "Nope, sorry just, had a rush of heat. You know how it is when you get older."

Her eyes narrowed. "You're like twenty-eight."

"Twenty-seven," I corrected. "Can't I have hot flashes at twenty-seven? Is that not a real thing?" I moved toward the espresso machine, putting objects between us before she figured out what was going on. "So the barbecue sounds fun."

"Nice subject change."

"Uh-huh." I grinned. "You want a coffee?"

"Decaf." She winked. "But Linc will have a triple shot Irish cream latte with extra foam."

My eyebrows shot up. "You know his drink well."

"Married." She laughed. "But I know how he likes everything. Remember I was his assistant for the summer? Best summer of his life."

Linc wrapped an arm around her and then nuzzled her neck. "Hell, yeah it was."

I tried not to sigh.

I failed.

They both gave me a funny look while I clutched the coffee cup to my bosom like I wished it was a baby.

"Coffee." I cleared my throat. "Coming right up."

By the time Linc and Dani left, I was able to clean up a bit and Jennifer was back to take over the afternoon shift.

My feet hurt from standing all day, so I put on another pair of Nikes and this time made sure that when I showed up at Trevor's house I didn't look homeless or like I was going to start digging through his trash for a snack. I was wearing a pair of black leggings and a cute red hoodie, and my hair was at least washed and pulled back into a sleek ponytail. I figured that as much as I wanted to show up in a gorgeous little black number that showed off my legs, that wouldn't be exactly the best way to nanny, especially after a day with those kids.

They were active, to say the least.

I was just getting ready to knock, giving myself a much needed extra few seconds to suck in oxygen so I didn't hold my breath in front of him or just gawk for longer than was socially acceptable, when the door jerked open. Trevor stood there, shirtless.

Again.

"Um…" I tilted my head and pointed. "Is this going to be a thing? You forgetting that you have muscles and I have eyes?"

His lips twitched. "In my defense, I was just victimized by three small children and finger paint."

"Let me guess, they thought you were a canvas?"

"Bingo!" He laughed and held the door open wider. "I shouldn't have confused them by wearing white."

"Tsk tsk, you amateur."

Trevor threw his head back and laughed. God, even his neck muscles were sexy. Must look anywhere but at the neck muscles and how they bulged above perfectly sculpted trap muscles.

The house looked pretty tidy, no laundry since I'd folded it the day before. Trevor's six pack flexed as he moved around the kitchen island then grabbed a black, vintage-looking shirt from the nearby chair and pulled it over his head. It had holes in it, but I think it was on purpose and if not, at least it was clean.

For being a rock star he was pretty low key about what he wore.

"All right." Trevor kissed Bella on the forehead, followed by Malcom and then Eric, who held up his fist for a bump. "Kids, be good for Penny, okay?"

Did he just drop the nickname again?

I told my heart to stop making such loud beats against my chest as he finally walked by me with a smile.

Calm down. It's not like you get a goodbye kiss too, stupid heart.

He stopped right in front of me. A foot away. My smile felt too wide, too forced. This was what I got for staying up late the night before and YouTubing footage from his most recent tour.

Footage of sweat running down his chest while he tossed his drumsticks into the crowd, footage of him crooning into the microphone as women screamed all around him, holding up posters, flowers, bras.

Trevor put his hands lightly on my shoulders. "You okay today?"

"Huh? Me? Yup. I'm great." I rocked back on my heels. "Sorry, it was just a busy day. Dani's back in town, and she stopped by…" Why was I even telling him this? It wasn't like he'd asked about my day.

I shut up when he grinned at me like I was being cute.

Right, so cute that I work at a coffee shop and smell like beans.

"I'm great," I repeated.

"Did you need a ride?" he asked.

"Ride?" What was he talking about? "To?"

His grin was so sexy I wanted to either kiss him or just take a picture and stare at it later under my covers. I needed to get a grip or I was going to lose touch with reality, wasn't I?

And reality was, at this moment, Trevor.

My job was not to stare at him and daydream, it was to do a job, to take care of his kids, to make sure that the hole their mother left in their hearts hurt less when I was around.

"The barbecue." He checked his watch and then looked back up to me. "We're headed over there too. In fact, I think—"

The doorbell rang.

He ran over and opened the door.

My jaw dropped.

I needed someone to physically move my chin back up, because while my brain was firing and telling me that it was time to close my mouth—it still refused to do it.

"Uncle Drew!" Bella went running.

I nearly died of shock when Drew knelt down, picked up Bella into his arms, and swung her around. Tattoos took up every inch of space down both arms, his ears were pierced, and I'm pretty sure he had a stud in his nose. He was beautiful, massive, and in the living room just, breathing in the same air.

Trevor laughed. "She's missed you."

"Everyone misses me." Drew barked out a laugh. "All right, Bells, I gotta go record some music with your dad, but I'll see you later at the barbecue, okay?"

"Okay!" She kissed his cheek and then patted where she kissed, her face lit up. "Oh, does that mean that Penny gets to come?"

"Did you get a cat?" Drew laughed as his eyes searched the room and then fell on me. His eyebrows rose straight up his forehead as he looked between me and Trevor. Bella ran full speed toward me, and I had no choice but to pick her up and let her little arms strangle me to death while both gorgeous men watched.

"Apparently that's my cue." I let out a weak laugh. "I would be the cat though I'm more like the nanny and I'd like to think that watching me in a cat video would be the opposite of entertaining. You know, since I don't have an obsession with goldfish and needing to be petted."

Too far. I just went too far, didn't I?

"You're funny." Bella squeezed me harder. "Can we play Barbies today?"

"Absolutely! Should we dress Eric up as Ken?"

"I WILL NOT!" Eric yelled, earning another laugh from us.

And Drew still stared.

Trevor cleared his throat…obviously, so obviously I wanted to die.

"Sorry." Drew took two steps toward me. "You're just not the vision that comes to mind when someone says nanny."

"Because I'm young?" I asked honestly.

"Because you're hot." He winked.

"And that's our cue." Trevor shoved Drew toward the door, only to have Drew poke his head back in.

"Number?" he called.

"Off limits," Trevor said in an annoyed voice.

"Name?" Drew kept trying and Trevor kept shoving.

I rolled my eyes and hugged Bella tighter. "Sorry. I don't give my name or number to strangers, right, Bella?"

"Stranger danger nine-one-one!" she shouted.

"Taught her that yesterday." I grinned and returned his wink.

It was Trevor's turn to poke his head around the corner of the door frame as he tried to shove Drew backwards. "Remind me to give you a raise."

"Oh, I will," I joked. "Go make music!"

"You should—" Drew sputtered as Trevor stepped in front of him, shutting down his attempt to linger by body blocking him out the door. "Son of a bitch!"

"Children!" Trevor shouted.

"Fine, fine, bye, sexy nanny, bye, beautiful Bella, later boys!" Drew yelled before the door slammed and I was left alone with all the kids.

Bella patted my cheeks with her chubby hands. "Your face is red."

"I'm hot," I said lamely.

Her face fell. "You can't marry Uncle Drew."

"Wait, what? Why would I marry Uncle Drew?"

"He called you sexy." She lowered her voice to a loud toddler whisper. "Sexy! Daddy says that means you have to get married!"

"Oh, honey." Bless her heart. "Trust me, I'm not marrying Uncle Drew."

"Oh, good." She sighed happily. "Because I already prayed that you would marry Daddy, and then there was a shooting star and Daddy says that means it's going to happen!"

Tears filled my eyes. I didn't have to heart to tell her I stopped praying and wishing on stars a long time ago.

Who was I to trample on her dreams anyways? "I guess we'll see."

With that, we walked toward the shouting between Eric and Malcom.

And within seconds, I had blue paint both somehow in my mouth and in my hair.

Yeah, I was totally going to marry a rock star.

Not.

Chapter Eight

Trevor

"Shut up." My first words once we got into the Escalade and drove toward the recording studio.

"Hmm?" Andrew cupped his ear. "I'm sorry, what was that? Were you just telling me to shut up? I didn't say anything."

I snorted and took a right toward downtown, the only downtown Seaside had with enough ice cream shops and taffy shops to make a lot of dentists very happy for a very long time.

"Your look says it all." I groaned. "For the record, I was desperate for someone to help with the kids, I came here to escape, to produce, to help lay tracks for the next album, and I've gotten shit done." I pulled into my parking space at the studio and killed the engine only to see Drew giving me the most shit-eating grin I'd ever seen—which really was saying a lot since the prick rarely smiled and up until recently had been on a downward spiral that would make any rock star proud.

"Fine." Drew grabbed his bag and then ran a hand through his buzzed hair. "All I'm saying is that she's hot as f—"

"Please don't finish that sentence."

"She's hot." Drew sighed like I was being unreasonable. "I mean you have to admit at least that. I can understand being desperate but did you have to hire someone that looks like she could be a super model as your nanny?"

I had no response.

Because what could I say that hadn't already been said?

She was beautiful.

She was working under my roof.

And she was taking care of my kids.

I let out a rough exhale. "We texted."

"OMG!" Drew yelled mockingly as he shoved a fist into my shoulder. "Did she make a pot roast for you too? And put on a maid outfit after—holy shit!" He burst out laughing. "This is the best day of my life. Tell me it was actually pot roast." He grabbed his phone and started texting. "This goes in the group text right the hell now."

"Don't!" I lunged for his phone, but he jumped out of the car and ran toward the studio, both fingers going at it.

My phone pinged.

Once, twice. Fucking perfect.

I was almost afraid to look.

Drew: RED ALERT 911 everyone drop their shit and listen up. Trevor has a hot nanny and she made him pot roast and wants to pot his roast.

Will: WHAT? Wait, hot nanny? Do we get to meet her? I'm in town for the BBQ and to record with you dumb asses.

Will was the core of our group. Next to Drew he sang the most on the tracks and was married to Linc's sister Angelica Greene, beautiful actress. Hah, been down that road, never again, just never again.

Me: Hilarious.

Ty: We need pictures. And pot your roast doesn't work bro, try again. I'll see you losers tonight.

At least Ty admitted to being a total jackass and man whore. The guy said settling down was too domesticated for his blood as proven with the harem of women that followed him around on a daily basis. That's what you get when you're one of the best guitarists in the world.

Laid.

Zane: I've never been more happy to be part of a text group. What about you, Linc? Alec? Demetri? Jaymeson?

Fantastic.

Shit for brains just had to add in rock duo AD2, superstar Zane "Saint" Andrews, and Jamie Jaymeson.

They were all friends.

All in the industry.

All completely settled down.

Which meant they fed off other people's drama like piranhas.

Demetri: We should make a home visit.

Alec: I'll bring pie since she made roast.

Jaymeson: The kids like her? Like they haven't burned the house down? Teach Alec your ways.

Alec: My kids make me tired. I've been tired for so long. Goodnight, Moon.

Linc: Terrifying also known as the day Alec Daniels says Goodnight Moon with tears in his eyes and actually means it.

Me: I'm leaving this group now, some guys have work to do.

Ty: See you tonight, bro!

Linc: I'm just going to say you're welcome in advance...the nanny will be there.

Demetri: There is a God.

Zane: Wow, I mean, like....what are you going to wear, Trev?

Drew: He smells like beans.

Me: Shut the hell up! Why are you texting me you're standing literal feet from me outside the studio!

Drew: And yet you're still in the car getting redder by the second, also don't wear that shirt, that shirt sucks.

Zane: No shirts. Clothing just takes too much time to take off anyways.

Demetri: Says the guy who never wears pants.

Jaymeson: And yet I send them to him every Christmas, he always follows with a nice picture of him burning them over a fire roasting marshmallows with a scarf around his naked body. Every year it's the same—except for the pants.

Alec: And his tiny pee-pee.

Zane: F U

Me: As fun as this has been, I'll see you guys tonight, be normal. Hell, what am I saying? Attempt not to scare other humans and for the love of God Zane, wear pants!

Zane: No promises.

I shoved my phone back into my pocket, got out of the Escalade, and glared at Drew. "Did you have to do that?"

"Oh, it was completely necessary." Drew chuckled. "Now let's go make some music and we can talk about this horrible T-shirt with its holes and how it's not going to impress HN."

"HN?" I repeated.

"Hot Nanny, keep up." He shoved me, I shoved him. All in all a normal day, because when I'm with my kids I feel like an adult, but when I'm with my bandmates and friends? I literally lose maturity points and years off my life.

I would never admit how much I needed it.

Especially after the divorce.

And being alone.

I was suddenly even more thankful Linc and Dani got pregnant and came back here, forcing the whole crew to come back into town early.

It was just supposed to be Drew and Ty for a week.

But now it was the entire gang.

Yeah, if Penelope survived the kids and this, she could survive anything.

"What's wrong with my shirt, though?" I lifted it and sniffed.

"If you have to sniff it to check, then you already know, bro." Drew laughed, and all thoughts of Penelope were gone as we set up and started playing.

It soothed me in a way nothing could.

I let the music lock on.

Closed my eyes.

And sang.

Five hours of bliss went by, five hours where I felt like my soul had finally relaxed into my own body once again, making the pain a little less, making the loss of someone I'd always counted on—dissipate.

"Sounds good," Drew said once we made it back to the house. His eyes weren't even on me, but on the door, staring a hole through it like he was seconds away from barging in and getting down on one knee.

"Your car." I jerked my head to the right. "See you at the barbecue, and try to stay away from my nanny, all right?"

He grinned, eying me up and down in that way that made me want to punch him in the face. Cocky bastard. "Ah, so now she's your nanny?"

"My kids'," I ground out while he choked on a laugh and started walking toward his waiting Range Rover.

"Tonight's gonna be fun!" he called, getting in while I flipped him off.

Bad timing on my part since I heard a little voice exclaim, "Why's Daddy showing his middle finger when he isn't driving?" I winced. Bella just had to be standing in the doorway with Penny.

Penny pressed her lips together then got down at eye level. "Well, probably because your Uncle Drew was driving."

"But he didn't go fast?" she countered.

Penny gave me a helpless look and smiled. "She heard the car pull up. The boys are upstairs fighting over who gets to wear Captain America, so good luck with that one."

I groaned and then lifted Bella into my arms once I reached the front door. Penelope's smile widened as she held the door open.

Everything was spotless.

I put Bella back on her feet and gaped. "How?"

"Soap," Penelope said with a smug grin.

"Smart ass," I said under my breath.

Bella giggled and looked up between us. "That's what Daddy calls Eric when he's in trouble. Are you in trouble, Penny?"

For some reason the question had me ready to launch a list of ways I could punish Penelope, ways I'd enjoy.

And I was astounded at how graphic my imagination got with my own daughter standing mere feet from me looking up at her new nanny like she owned a Barbie factory and worked at FAO Schwartz for the sole purpose of getting Bella new toys.

"No, sweetie." Penelope leaned down and kissed her head. "Hey, is it actually okay if I meet you guys there?"

Something in my chest deflated. Was I really that excited to take her to a barbecue?

"Um…" I scratched my head and forced a smile. "Yeah, I mean it starts in an hour so…"

"I can get ready fast." And then she leaned in and whispered in my ear, her lips so close to my skin I had trouble breathing. What the hell was wrong with me? "I smell like the wet dog your lovely children tried to rescue out back."

"Dog? We got a dog?"

"It was a small feral squirrel. It stepped in mud, then slipped on trash. I followed after it, and yeah, never mind. Point is, I should shower." She pulled away, our eyes locked.

And yet again, more visions of her peeling her shirt over her perfectly sculpted body, discovering what was underneath that hoodie seemed to be the only thing my worthless brain could focus on.

Water dripping down her skin.

She gulped and looked down while I wondered if Bella would notice if I touched the nanny.

Touched her?

Seriously?

Talk about crossing a line.

I took a step back, gathered my thoughts, and then nodded. "Yeah, that would be…a great idea."

"Told ya, I smell." She shrugged, her smile a bit wobbly, and then she was grabbing her purse and heading for the door.

I followed after her, not really sure why. It wasn't like it was dark yet and I was worried about her driving alone.

Maybe I just wanted to watch her.

Maybe I just wanted to have a few more seconds in her company.

Maybe I was losing my damn mind.

Chapter Nine

Penelope

"What the heck do I wear?" I wasn't panicking, not yet. I knew almost everyone except the members of Adrenaline.

Uncle Drew.

He'd been gorgeous.

And then there was Trevor, sexy-as-hell Trevor with his three kids and need to move on.

I'd completely planned on wearing what I'd had on, but after the squirrel incident, I wanted to at least make an effort.

And the way that Drew looked at me, well, quite honestly, it almost stung. I wanted Trevor to look at me that way, and then I mentally slapped myself and realized it wasn't about me.

It was about his kids.

I was an employee.

But that didn't mean I couldn't at least attempt something other than a hoodie.

Dani yawned. "I don't know, clothes?"

"Did you just yawn your answer?" I narrowed my eyes even though she wasn't there. "I have twenty minutes."

"And why are you suddenly so...concerned?" Her voice was way too amused, way too...knowing. Damn her.

"I'm ninety-nine percent sure I have some amount of squirrel feces on my person, that's why."

"I call false."

"Dani." I huffed and sat on my bed. "Help!"

"Who are we trying to impress?" At least this time she sounded more serious, more willing to help me do whatever the heck I was doing. Which was clothing myself and trying to appear like I had a steady job and knew how to take showers and use a razor.

"Humans. Let's just leave it at humans. And not the ones of the tiny variety with chocolate on their hands and love in their hearts." I smiled to myself. "Though I do love those kind too."

She was quiet and then. "You'll be a great mom one day."

"Yeah." My voice cracked. I didn't tell her the daunting truth, that not only did you have to have a man, but that the older I got, the more my chances died right along with my eggs. I wasn't even being dramatic, I was just being honest. I'd been the lucky recipient of HPV in high school, where it turned into the early stages of cervical cancer which meant that after all was said and done my chances of getting pregnant were a stellar five percent during my most fertile times.

Tears welled in my eyes.

I didn't want to focus on it.

I couldn't.

Because then I felt sorry for myself, and I resented everything and everyone, including the news whenever I saw someone who abandoned a kid or couldn't take care of them. I wanted to reach in and hold them close and sob.

"You still there?" Dani asked gently.

"Yeah." I swiped my cheeks, wondering when I'd started actually crying on the phone. "Maybe I'll just wear a pair of jeans?"

"Shorts," she corrected. "Jean cut-offs to be exact, a cute tank with a hoodie since it's still nice out, and a pair of sandals. You'll look great. Oh, and do your hair."

"I do my hair." I touched the ponytail on my head and winced as I realized most of my hair had pulled out of the actual ponytail.

"You never wear it down," she said accusingly. "And it's gorgeous and silky, and if you want to impress adult humans, ones that don't care that you smell like cheese, you should try that angle."

"Why do I call you again?"

"Because you love me?"

"True," I grumbled. "I might be a bit late."

"Even better!" She seemed amused by this, though I couldn't understand why unless she was banking on me tripping on my own feet and landing face down on someone's crotch. One time that happened. Friends and family never let me live it down. "See you soon!"

"Yeah." I hung up and stared down at my cut-off jean shorts. At least I'd already showered. "Well," I said to myself. "Here goes nothing."

Chapter Ten

Trevor

The only thing better than having a nanny who could prevent the house from being burned down? Other kids.

A miracle had taken place at that barbecue.

My kids ran off with the littler kids and neighbor kids, and cousins of friends, and honestly, at that point even if it was a complete stranger and their kids, I was okay with it. Especially if it made Eric laugh.

And that was exactly what was happening.

We were at Dani and Linc's beach house, which just so happened to have Jaymeson and Pris right next door, and on the other side was a family recently moved in from Seattle.

They had five kids under the age of seven.

And they were having a birthday party with live reptiles, which meant all three of my kids disowned me and ran over to join.

I exhaled probably for the first time in an hour and watched as one of Alec and Demetri's security detail slowly made their way over to the group and stood.

"You always keep him around?" I asked once Alec approached me. Tattoos lined his arms. He was a few years younger than me, but that meant shit in this industry. He and his brother had gone through a lot in the last few years. The fact that he was semi-unscathed was shocking.

He took a sip of water. "Yeah well, ever since Ella turned two we've been hounded by enough photographers to land me in prison and since Nat's pregnant again, I figured better safe than sorry, plus he's all bark no bite."

I followed his gaze.

The guy looked like he ate small children for breakfast. No smile. No hair. Enough muscles protruding from his body to look lethal. "Yeah, I guess I'll take your word for it."

Eric decided to choose that moment to grab the iguana and shove it in his face.

The security guy didn't even flinch.

"See?" Alec laughed. "He'll take care of them, plus the property's all gated. Enjoy the barbecue and the free time."

"Free time," I repeated. "What's that again?"

"A unicorn I can never seem to trap." Alec laughed just as his brother walked over with a shit-eating grin on his face. "I'm almost afraid to ask."

"Oh, you're fine." He turned his smirk on me. "You, on the other hand, are completely screwed."

"Now I'm afraid to ask," I grumbled. "Don't you have someone else to pester?"

Demetri laughed, his dimples showing on both sides as his messy blond hair fell over his tan face. "Actually no, I'm all free. The wife is with the rest of the wives in the kitchen talking with HN."

"Hot Nanny," Alec said helpfully in a low whisper.

"Got that," I said in a short voice. "Are you guys really that bored?"

"Yes," they said in unison.

"You're like the shiny new toy we get to make fun of and drown in the ocean, you're welcome." Demetri laughed just as Zane walked over, as promised, completely shirtless. The guy was labeled walking talking sex, and he oozed it everywhere he went—and often. Bastard.

"Can someone get him a shirt?" I mumbled as Zane flashed me a cheeky grin and winked. "NOW?"

"I'm good, Dad, thanks though." Zane crossed his arms. "So, HN is here, I had my phone ready to record your expression, but the girls confiscated it the minute they saw me smile."

"Color me shocked," Alec said dryly.

Zane flipped him off. "All right." He patted me on the back. "Remember, she's the nanny, that means hands off, yeah? She's teaching the next generation, under your protection, you're paying her to—"

"Holy shit," I muttered as Penelope walked out the sliding glass door with wine in one hand.

My mouth went completely dry.

Her tan legs went on for miles.

Her shorts were almost indecently short, or maybe it just felt indecent because I couldn't stop staring at all the tan skin.

Short, worn, brown cowboy boots added to the effect. Her white blouse was unbuttoned, revealing a teal swimsuit top, and a few necklaces danced between her breasts like they couldn't help but move against her supple skin. And her hair…

Down.

Her hair was down.

Under waves and waves of lush shots of brown, orange, and whiskey-colored strands—a smile peeked through at me, and then a small wave with her free hand.

"Say it with me." Zane wrapped an arm around me. "Off. Limits."

"Good, Zane." Demetri laughed. "Just wave a flag in front of a bull, why don't you? That's the easiest way to get—ohhhhh…" He nodded. "I see what you're doing. Carry on."

"Huh?" I looked back and forth between them. "What?"

"It's been too long." This time it was Alec that piped up. "You need to move on."

"Thanks, Dr. Phil." I gripped the beer bottle in my hand so tight I was surprised it didn't break in half, and then Drew chose that moment to walk up to Penelope and wrap an arm around her. Something he said made her laugh.

"She used to have a poster of us in her room," I blurted. "She said Drew was her favorite."

"Glorious Day!" Zane burst out laughing. "Then I suggest you start practicing with those handy drumsticks, because he's about one more joke away from touching a necklace and oh shit he's good."

My eyes widened as Drew picked up one of her necklaces and leaned in, inches from her face. She laughed again.

"I've never been so happy to be married," Alec announced. "That guy's lethal. No wonder the band broke up and Will got all pissed back in the day. He could charm the pants off a—"

"Stop," I said, gritting my teeth and running my hands through my hair.

"Well, off you go!" Demetri slapped me on the ass just as Linc made his way over, hands up.

"I saw nothing."

I flipped him off and passed Jaymeson as he manned the grill with Alec's wife; they were arguing over a movie. The closer I got to them the more irritated I became.

And I was in stunned disbelief that Drew would flirt with Penelope after my warning. What the hell was he thinking?

"Hey." My voice actually cracked. I inwardly punched myself in the dick and forced a cool smile. "Drew, Will just got here, he wanted to talk about some of the tracks."

Drew's grin was slow, steady. "Oh, yeah? Shouldn't you be there too? Since you're producing our next album? Plus I thought I saw Ty walk in and there he is." He waved our third bandmate over.

Ty swaggered in our direction. In ways he reminded me of Zane. He hated clothes and loved women.

All women.

All the time.

"Who's this?" He winked down at Penelope and then reached for her hand.

"DADDY!" Bella screamed.

Moment shattered, I turned in the direction of her voice and sprinted. One of the giant lizards had somehow managed to crawl over her lap and trap her.

The reptile handler was in the process of pulling the harmless creature away when I reached her side. The security guard tried helping her to her feet, which I assumed was the reason she began to scream "stranger danger nine-one-one." Thanks, Penny.

I pulled her into my arms and wiped the tears from her cheeks. "Are you okay, baby?"

"Yeah." She sniffled as giant alligator tears ran down her puffy cheeks. "I gots scared and then Eric didn't help me. Aren't brothers supposed to help?"

Eric was pale next to Malcom, who looked like he was ready to puke.

The lizard had been huge; they were probably scared too.

"That's why you have a daddy," I answered in a hoarse voice. "So that when your brothers get scared too, I'm here. I'll always be here, all right?"

"You keep me safe." She sniffled again. "Right, Daddy?"

God, my heart was breaking in half.

How was I supposed to do this?

Navigate this life? Keep them safe? From everything? From things that weren't supposed to hurt them—like their own mother?

"Of course he does," came a familiar voice.

And then Bella was reaching for Penelope, and I was letting my little girl go into her arms as she rocked her back and forth. "That's what family does, we protect one another, we love one another, and when scary things happen, it's not because your daddy lets them happen or your brothers, sometimes they just…do, but that's why it's so important to be brave and strong, all right?"

Bella nodded then put her sticky hands on Penelope's cheeks. "Are you brave and strong, Penny?"

I didn't miss the tears in Penny's eyes as she nodded and then slowly said, "I try very hard, but you know what makes me feel brave and strong?"

Bella shook her head.

"You." They touched foreheads. "Because look! That lizard was like two of you! And you did the right thing. You yelled for your daddy. You only cried a little bit and now, now we can have cake, right?"

"Cake!" Bella squeezed her neck.

Penny let her down as all the kids started running toward the picnic table. It was only a few feet away from the fence to the backyard barbecue. All the kids gathered around the table singing, leaving me and Penny alone with the reptiles, a keeper, and a worried-looking security guard.

I wasn't sure why I did it.

Maybe one day it would occur to me not to just act on impulse when it came to women.

But I grabbed her hand.

I squeezed it.

I didn't let go.

And neither did she.

I wasn't sure how long we stood like that, hand in hand, watching the kids eat cake like it was the most interesting thing on the planet.

But we did.
Two adults.
Two very different worlds.
United by one very similar love.
My children.

Chapter Eleven

Penelope

The feel of his palm against mine would be forever imprinted on my mind. It wasn't a normal hand holding.

It felt...personal.

Raw.

It felt like something I never wanted to share with anyone else. Even the thought of talking about it out loud seemed to take away the specialness of it.

We hadn't talked about it.

Bella had at one point looked over at us and smiled.

And then Eric had promptly thrown cake at Malcom's face, shattering the moment as Trevor sighed and went. "Looks like I'm up."

I helped him clean up Malcom and made my way back to the barbecue to grab a plate of food. Bella came with me and Eric trailed behind.

"I hope he's paying you overtime for this," Drew said as he handed me a plate and then took Bella out of my arms and held her.

I frowned. "Overtime? What are you talking about?"

Drew gave me an odd look. He'd been telling me funny stories about Trevor and the rest of the band on the road, stories that made me greedy for more Trevor, which was basically the worst idea on the planet at this point. I was already getting too attached, wasn't I?

"Bella, why don't you go sit next to Uncle Will and Aunt Angelica for a bit? You too, Malcom." Drew said. They both sprinted in the opposite direction. I made sure they actually listened to him and then faced Drew in curiosity.

"Look." He licked his full lips. "It's a good thing, what you're doing for Trevor. I just don't want him to take advantage of you."

"Take advantage," I repeated, feeling almost embarrassed. "I like the kids, love them actually. I was a teacher. I've always loved kids, and he needs help. That's all this is. Plus, I don't really think about it as a job, you know?"

His eyes widened. "You do realize they set their last nanny on fire?"

I laughed.

He joined in and shook his dark hair. "Yeah, you should get hazard pay."

"They're harmless." I shrugged as Malcom tripped over his own feet and face planted in his hot dog. It fell onto the grass, Will picked it up and dusted it off then made a face at Malcom, which I'm sure prevented Malcom from crying.

"So harmless," Drew echoed. "So, should we go out?"

My smile dropped as I turned and frowned at him. "I'm sorry, what?"

"On a date." He shoved his hands in his pockets. "Food's usually involved, intelligent conversation on both sides, possibly more on yours, since I like to hear your voice. What do you say?"

"No," Trevor's voice answered for me. "She says no."

Drew gave him a murderous look. "No offense, man, but she's the nanny, not your girlfriend."

I flinched.

I hated that he was right.

"Exactly," Trevor said through clenched teeth. "My kids' nanny, my employee, which means hands off."

"Funny." Drew crossed his arms.

"What?"

"You should listen to yourself and then go take a long hard look in the mirror. Just because you can't have her doesn't mean you can keep her away from someone who could." He smirked at both of us and then saluted Trevor with his middle finger and walked off toward Ty and Linc.

"Sorry about that," Trevor murmured. "He means well."

I turned and glared. "I get that you're my boss, but that doesn't mean you get to dictate what I do off the clock, right?"

His eyes widened. "Yes. No. I mean—" He gulped. "He's a player. He's not good, not for you."

I pressed my lips together. "And that's your call to make because...?"

He stared me down, his eyes heated.

I almost backed away.

But I was frustrated.

Frustrated that Drew was right.

Frustrated that he saw right through it all.

Frustrated that Trevor was the kind of guy who would stay in a perpetual state of sexual frustration before acting on anything.

"I need a drink," he finally muttered before leaving me standing there, alone and wondering where it all went wrong between the hand holding and the arguing.

Stewing, I sat on the nearest chair, only to have Will plop right down next to me. How was this my life? That the lead singer, one of the most famous guys in the world, was suddenly sitting next to me eating potato chips and shooting the breeze. I mean, I'd been surrounded by a lot of these guys but this was next level.

All of them were A list.

Every last one.

No B list allowed, it seemed.

"So," Will exhaled. "All I'm going to say is this, he feels everything."

"What?" I craned my neck.

Will was wearing glasses, which just added to the GQ effect of his tight ripped jeans and black tank. He had bracelets wrapped around each wrist and a wedding ring on his left ring finger. It was the only part about him that looked domesticated. The guy had gone into hiding it seemed and then came back on the scene with his entire band spouting out Grammys like they'd never taken any time off, except to turn into men with muscles and killer smiles.

The world wasn't ready.

I wasn't ready.

"Trevor." Will leaned forward, resting his forearms on his thighs. "He feels everything. Most musicians do. I swear none of us can even have a crush without falling so hard that it's almost embarrassing. It's all or nothing with us, we all grew up on the road, didn't experience life the way normal people do. When we dated, it was almost always famous people who wanted something from us. Normal was crashing someone's prom for a TV show, normal was finishing high school on a tour bus, normal was snorting cocaine before the show so we didn't fall asleep on stage. What I'm saying is, he doesn't react the same way a normal guy would because he's not normal. None of us are, and if you think we are, then you're lying to yourself. You've known Linc for a while, you've known Alec and Demetri just as long. You forget how famous they are because they're like family. You're in this little cocoon of Seaside or, what was it? Wyoming? Montana?"

I made a face.

He just laughed. "Walk down the street with him, just once. Not during the morning when everyone is still getting up, but at night, rush hour, watch the stares he gets, the pictures people ask to take. His life isn't his own. And the sick part is that he's right in the middle of one of the biggest divorce scandals to hit Hollywood, and you're sitting there wondering why he can't just step out on a ledge and do more than hold your hand—"

"I wasn't..." Shame washed over me. Because he was right.

"All it takes is one picture of holding your hand and you're in this, and he's known you what? A few days? And you want him to do something stupid like ask you on a date? We aren't all Drew."

I smiled at that. "Drew seems the most carefree."

"Because he's in the most pain." Will looked away. "I know we don't know each other, I just didn't want you to think it was you or that there was anything wrong with you. This is a legit not-you-but-him scenario. Do yourself a favor, all right?"

"What?" I leaned forward.

"Just be there for him. Watch the kids, make sure they don't set you on fire like the last one, and be there for him. And if you like Drew, go out with Drew. Nobody's stopping you."

"But Trevor said—"

"Trevor's still in love with his ex-wife," Will said softly. "She's the mother of his children, and it's been a year. If you like Drew, go out with him. And let Trevor just...figure his shit out."

"So basically you're explaining to me in the kindest way that you can—"

"It won't work, not right now, Penelope."

"You're the oldest, aren't you?" I smiled over at him. "Like the patriarch of the band?"

"Patriarch makes me sound old. Do I really look that old?" He grinned.

I burst out laughing. "No, if anything, it's like you guys are aging backwards."

"Happens when you make a deal with a vampire." He stood, and then leaned over and kissed me on the top of my head. "For what it's worth, I think you'd be exactly what he needs."

"But?"

"But." He shrugged. "Timing's a real bitch."

"Yeah," I croaked.

And locked eyes with Trevor as he took a swig of beer. He didn't look away, just stared me down like he could see my soul.

Seconds later, Drew was blocking my view of Trevor, and he was grinning like he already knew what I was going to say.

"Let me guess, you changed your mind?" He tilted his head with a beautiful smile spreading across his face.

"Maybe." My eyes narrowed. "But just as friends."

His face fell.

"You do know what that is right?"

"You're killing me."

"You'll be fine." I patted him on the shoulder. "Besides, you don't want me."

"What makes you say that?"

"The heart wants what it wants." I grinned. "And I'm pretty sure the last thing on this planet you want is to settle down."

His eyebrows shot up as he leaned in and whispered against my ear, "Wrong."

Chapter Twelve

Trevor

"Thanks again," I whispered to Penelope as we put the last of the kids in their bedroom. She must have seen the exhaustion on my face because she offered to ride back with me and help get them ready for bed. Eric and Malcom were like zombies. Penny took one look at them, scooped up Bella, and announced that she was going to help me get them tucked in, which naturally earned a curious look from every single person at the barbecue. After all, she was going above and beyond but anyone with eyes could see it was because she just had a big heart.

Plus, according to Drew, she'd said yes.

According to Will, I needed to let it go.

According to my heart and mind, I didn't want to let go of shit. I wanted to ask her why, I wanted to thump my head against the wall until things made sense, until I knew what to do.

In all the scenarios I'd considered in my head, I'd never once gone over the idea that I could be so quickly attracted to another woman after all the baggage I'd had heaped on my shoulders.

I mean, three kids was intimidating enough, but she took it in stride.

I was a single dad.

But Penny didn't treat me that way.

"Night, Bella." Penny kissed her on the forehead. I followed suit, turned on her unicorn light, and shut the door. The house was too quiet, almost eerily quiet as we both slowly walked down the stairs and into the kitchen.

"I appreciate that." I yawned behind my hand. "Did you want anything to drink?"

"I'm good." Penny smiled. "I'll just call an Uber real quick or something."

I snickered at that. "Was that your plan all along?"

She made a funny face. "Well, yeah. Everyone has—" She stopped herself. "Why are you looking at me like that?"

"Because." I grinned harder. "It's Seaside, you'd have better luck corralling a seagull and riding it back to your place."

She groaned. "I have to get up at five a.m."

"Stay here." The words were out before I could stop them. "I mean, in one of the guest rooms, not my room because that would be—" Idiot, I was going to drown myself in the nearest body of water and stay there forever. "—weird. I'll just grab you a towel if you want to shower, not that you need to. You smell great." Good Trev, good, tell her how good she smells again.

She suppressed a smile.

I shook my head. "I think after each kid the universe just took cool points away from my person and replaced them with dad points. I swear I'm not trying to make myself look like an ass or make you uncomfortable."

Penny nodded. "I know, and if it makes you feel any better I don't think I was ever gifted with any cool points. I mean, I can't play an instrument, and my gift is making coffee."

"The greatest gift of them all," I pointed out with a nod.

"Hah!"

The lights flickered.

She gave me a worried look, her eyes darting from me to the lights and back again.

"It's fine, it's probably just starting to storm a bit. I've been told it's normal around this time of year."

She worried her lower lip and nodded. "All right, I may just take you up on that offer..."

My eyebrows shot up.

"Towel. Separate bed. That sort of thing." She waved her hand awkwardly and dropped it at her side.

It was my turn to smile. "This way." I led her to the guest room on the second level. It might as well be a mother-in-law suite. Even though it was still connected to the main part of the house, it had its own kitchen and was large enough to rent out if I ever wanted to. The walls were bare and white, not graced by so much as a sconce or a big box store version of a Picasso print. There was one queen-sized bed sporting a beige comforter on the west end of the room beneath a window with beige mini-blinds and no curtains. Two bedside tables flanked the bed, each occupied by a generic crystal and pewter lamp with crinkled beige shades. A flat-screen TV took up most of the wall opposite the bed, and a small, mirrored dresser hugged the side wall across from the door.

The room really, truly needed to be decorated, but I hadn't found the time.

"Wow!" She did a small circle. "This is great!"

"Yeah, it is." I couldn't take my eyes off of her; this was a problem.

The lights flickered again.

Like the universe was trying to do me a solid.

Everything went out, blanketing us in darkness.

I hated it because I couldn't see her.

I loved it because I could still feel her.

Everywhere.

"Okay, the pretty room just got a bit terrifying." Her voice was weak. "I'm a wimp, I'm sorry, I don't even like living alone, but I was like, you know what I should do? Move across the country and start fresh, because I've lived in the same town my whole life, with the same roommate, working at the same school doing the same thing over and over again and you know what the definition of that is?" She finally took a breath. "Insanity."

"That was a long sentence."

"I know." She exhaled roughly and then her hands were on my chest. She jerked them back. "Sorry. I was trying to find something to hold on to, not someone, just, like a wall to steady myself or—"

"I'll steady you," I whispered.

This was bad.

All of it.

I saw her worried face once again as lightning flickered outside. And then it was just us, blanketed in the silent buzz of awareness pulsing between our two bodies.

I'd known her days.

I'd focused on those days instead of the nights.

Because the nights were full of wondering what she tasted like.

Wondering if this would be different if I wasn't a plus three.

I was afraid to move.

Afraid that if I slid my hand up her arm and cupped her chin, she'd pull away from me, from the kids.

How damn selfish could I be?

It wasn't just me.

They needed her more than I did.

I took a step back and let out a rough exhale. "I'll go grab you a flashlight, all right?"

"I can't see you, don't go!" Her voice sounded so small.

Reminding me what it felt like to feel needed, and maybe just a little bit wanted too.

I reached out, touching first her shoulder then slowly running my hand down until I found her hand and squeezed it.

She squeezed it back tight.

And I wanted to stay in the darkness and just…exist in that place where uncertainty made me brave enough to hold her hand, and certainty didn't glare its ugly head and tell me that this would never happen, not in a million years.

"We can go together," I offered, pulling out my cell with my free hand. "That way you're not alone."

She nodded.

When I turned on my cell light, I flicked it to her face briefly. "You have yours on you?"

She reached into her back pocket and pulled out her phone.

Both of us pointed them down the hallway, and we made our way into the master. I didn't want to make her uncomfortable but I kept two flashlights under my bed just in case. It was a dad thing, a keep the kids safe in case of an emergency thing.

I quickly grabbed one and handed it to her. "Here you go."

"Why do you keep flashlights under your bed?" she asked. Her voice was a lot more calm, which made me relax a bit as she switched on the light and pointed it around the room. "Wow, this is…beautiful."

Everything was draped in rich blues and browns. It *was* beautiful. It was mine, the only place that the kids knew was off limits when it came to bedtime, though lately they'd been trying to crash with me even though they knew it was my inner sanctum. Typically if they needed me, I slept in their beds, held their hands, cradled their tiny bodies.

I found myself explaining. "Kids take over…everything. They're like lovable chaotic tornados." I shrugged and smiled over at Penny even though the flashlight wasn't pointed at me but was still bouncing around the enormous master suite. "When we moved here, I wanted to keep something—anything—that was just mine, that reminded me that it would get better. That one day I'd be able to share a room like this with someone who got it, who got us, who accepted us, loved us, who wanted to share this with us."

The flashlight dropped out of her hand. "Sorry!"

I helped her pick it up, my hand draped across hers.

I jerked back like I'd been burned.

Slowly we both stood.

I knew she was close.

I could smell her, feel her as if we were sharing air, sharing heartbeats, maybe even sharing thoughts.

The pull was so intense I couldn't think straight.

I purposely pointed the flashlight to the floor and cupped her chin. Our foreheads touched. I could feel her pulse, would have sworn I could hear it, hear her heart hammer against her ribs, hear the sharp intake of breath as I leaned down and pressed a kiss to her mouth.

I knew it was wrong.

Every single rational thought told me it was the worst idea I'd ever had. But she made me feel needed. And I hadn't realized how much I'd craved that since Jo left us, left me, making me feel inadequate in any and every way a woman knew how.

Penny's lips parted.

Her flashlight dropped again, but this time it was because she was wrapping her arms around my neck.

I pulled her against me, our mouths met, and we nipped at each other. My lips slid against hers in a way that was so erotic, I was having trouble thinking straight. She was so open to me, so damn beautiful, even in the darkness. I could feel her beauty; it wasn't the way she looked.

I felt her heart.

She let out a little moan as I dove my free hand into her hair, followed by tracing my tongue across her lower lip. She let out a little gasp that had her body pressing harder against mine.

Blood pounding.

It would be too easy.

It had been over a year, and even before that Jo and I hadn't been sleeping in the same room.

Too long.

And now I had Penny.

Perfect Penny.

And a bed.

Alone.

In the darkness.

The lights flickered.

And then they were on.

Penny jerked away from me, chest heaving.

I had trouble catching my breath.

I wasn't sure how long we stared at each other. What I was sure of? That I had made those cheeks pink, I had made those lips swell. And I wanted to do it again.

"Daddy?" Bella's voice sounded at the door. "Is it a storm?"

"Yeah, baby," I said in a raspy voice. "It's a good one though."

"How do you know?" She padded over to me, then reached up. I pulled her into my arms and smiled while Penny still seemed frozen in shock.

"Well…" I grinned at her then looked over at Penny as I whispered, "Sometimes the dark makes us brave, and that makes the storm good, not bad."

Penny bit down on the lip I'd just tasted and then grabbed the flashlight with a shaky hand and placed it on my bed. "I'll just…be heading to bed."

"You're staying!" Bella squealed, "Please sleep in my room! Please! I have princess bunk beds."

I opened my mouth to say no.

Instead Penny beamed. "Actually, I'd love that, let's go!"

"Follow me!" Bella scrambled from my embrace and bolted out the door.

"Using my daughter as a human shield?" I whispered under my breath.

Penny crossed her arms and stared me down. "Maybe."

"Are you still going out with Drew later?"

"Does it matter?" she fired back.

"Yes. No. Maybe." I gulped and ran my hands through my hair. "He's just…"

"The kind of guy that kisses the nanny?" she whispered, her cheeks going pink again.

"Penny, no, that's not…"

She just shrugged and left me alone in that room.

Wondering how the hell I was going to fix it.

Because the reality was, I had all the power in the situation. I was paying her to watch my kids, to keep them alive; I was paying her as an employee. I'd basically just kissed my employee and had been seconds away from lifting her shirt over her head or just ripping it from her body.

And she was going to be on a date with Drew.

Drew, the same guy who had slept his way through Austin, Texas.

Twice.

What could go wrong?

Chapter Thirteen

Penelope

Fact. I'd let it happen.

Fact. I'd known it would happen.

Fact. I hadn't pulled away.

Fact. I'd liked it.

I'd called Fallon the next morning freaking out and she still had the same sage advice as before, adventure, let it happen, agh!

"Wow, I don't think I've ever been on a date with a girl who stared so hard at a burger." Drew shoved a fry into his mouth and then took a sip of his beer.

Mine was untouched.

Because I was still thinking about the kiss.

The kiss that shouldn't have happened.

The words before the kiss about wanting to share his life with someone who got it.

And the little crack in my heart that seemed to open even more as I realized I wanted exactly the same thing. I'd never been the sort of girl who wanted anything huge.

A family.

A real family.

Was that so much to ask for?

According to Trevor, no. And that was the thing, he was famous, but still so normal in the desires of his heart. It made him so maddeningly attractive that I couldn't even hold a conversation during my date with Drew.

It didn't help that things had gone back to normal with Trevor, I had dinner waiting for him the last three nights, he greeted me with a huge smile when I showed up at one, usually with some sort of food substance on his person, and on and on we went, in perfect sync, around one another, laughing about the kids.

But not acting on anything.

We were never alone.

Maybe that was a good thing.

Yeah, my stomach dropped and then filled with erratic butterflies, all hell bent on escaping, at once.

A very good thing.

"Sorry." I picked up a fry and shoved it in my mouth. "I just have a lot on my mind."

"Right, because making coffee is basically the same thing as solving world hunger. Not that I'm hating on your job, we all need coffee. You're basically a saint to us sinners, but tell me one thing." He sat forward. The guy had such lethal eyes, so piercing and deep that no sane person could look away. "What sort of answers do you think you're going to find on an empty stomach?"

"Ah, so basically if I eat my food, I'll be all powerful?"

"Well." His smirk widened as he leaned in and whispered. "They are fries."

I narrowed my eyes. "Be honest, are you here because you want to be here, because you're bored, or because you want to piss off Trevor by feeding his employee?"

His expression fell a bit and then he leaned back and crossed his arms. He had bracelets on both wrists, the colorful rope kind that his bandmates seemed to collect since most of them were covered in them. His black V-neck went down so low I could see half his chest tattoo. His fingernails were painted black, and I was almost positive he had eyeliner on, unless that was real, and he really did have such intense eyes. If it was, not fair, not fair to any of us.

Drew had always been the bad boy of the group.

The one that every girl said they loved but never chose to marry when it came to playing the whole kiss, date, marry game.

No, the marry one had always been Trevor.

He was sexy but good. Heck, the guy did interviews while holding puppies.

"Can't I just share a nice meal with a nice person?"

I almost choked on my fry. "You don't know me."

"And you don't know me," he countered with narrowed eyes.

I opened my mouth then shut it and glared.

"That's why we have the food." He spread his arms wide. "Calories are supposed to make it easier."

"And yet…" I laughed and took another swig of beer.

"And yet, most people don't even eat because they feel like puking." He gulped and then looked away. "And it may have something to do with having to clean up my image for the next album."

"That—" I pointed a fry at him. "—makes total sense." I grinned. "Maybe you should start doing volunteer work."

The guy visibly paled.

"Or not." I snickered.

"Music." He said the word like it was sexy. No, he said it like it was actually dripping with sex. "It's all I need."

"Until you wake up alone," I whispered under my breath.

"Oh, sweetheart, I'm never alone." He let out a laugh.

"I'm calling your bluff."

His smile fell. "Don't you scour the internet? See the magazines?"

"Yeah, but I don't pay attention to that." I leveled a serious stare on him. "And even if you do have some crazy fan girl in your bed every night, that doesn't mean you're never alone. You can be surrounded by millions of people, friends, family, fans—and still be lonely."

I wasn't sure where that came from.

Maybe the part inside of me that had always felt that way, like it didn't quite fit, and that everyone else did back in Cunningham Falls.

Another reason to move to Seaside.

To find my place.

My destiny.

Drew was quiet as he stared down at his fries, and then he leaned back in his chair again, reached for his beer and downed it to the last drop. "Well, at least now I know why."

"Why you're lonely?" I asked, confused.

"Nah." He flashed me a smile that seemed almost disappointed. "Why he likes you so much, why he's so protective of you."

"He barely knows me." My mind flashed to the kiss, to the days spent with his kids getting to know him through them, dinners spent at his house. One week in, and I was ready to ask if I should just become their live-in nanny and pine after him for the rest of my life.

If that wasn't crazy, I wasn't sure what was.

"Maybe you should share more food with him," Drew offered. "Wait, you're already doing that. Don't you make a killer pot roast?"

"Very funny." I tilted my head at him, my eyes searching his expression. "I'm trying to figure out your angle here, and I keep coming up empty."

"Maybe—" He gulped and licked his lips. "Maybe I just need a friend too."

"Lonely notices lonely," I whispered.

"Yeah," was all he said before waving his hand to our waiter. We were at one of Seaside's brewery joints, it had killer food but suddenly the few fries and conversation sat like a rock in my stomach.

I once again felt like I didn't fit.

I wanted to.

It would be easy to like someone like Drew.

To fall for his easy smiles and smoldering eyes.

But it was wrong.

It felt wrong.

And Trevor's hands felt right, his mess felt right. All the way down to the ketchup stains and the crazy looks his kids gave me whenever I asked them to help with anything.

"She did a number on him, you know." Drew tossed a wad of cash on the table and stood. "His ex."

"Who abandons three kids?" I wondered out loud as we walked out of the restaurant, his hand on the small of my back. He had flat-out refused to let me meet him there, so I walked over to the passenger side of his Range Rover and waited.

A few people held up their phones around us, but it wasn't anything crazy. Then again, it wasn't tourist season yet.

I couldn't even imagine what they dealt with during the summertime if they were walking down the streets with all the normal humans who didn't have pretty tattoos and gorgeous faces.

Drew opened my door for me and didn't answer until we were in the car. And then he just shook his head and started the engine. "A very,

very selfish person. And trust me when I say I know some of the worst. We're from LA, it's like the capital of consumerism and narcissists, but it's—I don't know, it's worse than that. She actually made him believe she wanted that life, and the minute he gave her everything she wanted, it wasn't enough. It's like this switch flipped when she realized it wasn't always going to be glamorous parties and Grammy awards." Drew sighed. "The worst thing you can do when you're famous…" He pulled up to a stoplight and turned his gaze toward me. "…is to date or marry someone in the same business, who feels the need to compete with you. I'd like to think they can't help it, it's a competitive business. But she had one or two hit movies, he's had a career since he was thirteen that kept thriving. And he was willing to walk away from it when all she wanted was more, more, more." The light turned green and he accelerated again. "The addiction isn't in the first taste, Penelope, it's in the justification that all you need is one, when you will always need more to replace what's been consumed."

I stared at him slack-jawed.

His lips turned up into a smile. "And the bad boy of the group just got deep. Sorry…sometimes I forget I'm supposed to be stupid."

I laughed at that. "You're not stupid."

"No, I just like to hide my smarts behind my body, easier to get laid that way."

"There you are." I laughed.

He joined me, and then he was pulling up to my house. My tiny little beach house with the cute red door, painted white window boxes for flowers, and Jennifer standing in the middle of my lawn with her cell pressed to her ear and her hands in the air in frustration.

I was renting from Jennifer and her family. Since it was close to the coffee shop, it just made sense. But she'd never actually visited me or stood on my lawn at night looking crazed.

I got out of the SUV.

Drew followed me. Of course he did.

"Jennifer?"

She turned and then held up a hand. "Well, fix it! I have a tenant!"

She ended the call and gave me a frustrated look. "I'm so sorry, Penelope, one of the neighbors smelled smoke and called the fire department. There's no fire, but the power outage earlier today apparently caused a whole bunch of craziness with the old wiring in the house. Old wiring that was supposed to be fixed last year. The electrical contractor claimed we had a few more years left, so we didn't do anything and…" She looked ready to cry. "I'm so sorry, but it's not safe right now. Is there any place you can stay for the next week or so?"

"Um…" Panic set in. Well, it wasn't actually *setting* in, I was already in full-fledged panic mode. I didn't want to ruin Dani and Linc's time here. Though I knew they had a huge beach house, I just hated imposing on anyone.

Hated the idea that I'd be dependent again.

That I wouldn't fit.

Why did I always feel like I was floating in limbo? Just waiting to be told this path, this one right here, take it!

"I have a place," Drew announced.

I sent him a seething glare. "I'm not staying with you."

He burst out laughing. "Wasn't offering, not really into girls who see too much. That's why we get to be friends and I'm helping you hurry things along. Just call me your fairy fucking godmother!"

I could have sworn my eye started to twitch.

Jennifer gasped when she realized who he was, then dropped her phone onto the grass. Then she bent and scooped it up and asked for a selfie. Then she looked ready to burst into tears all at once.

Yeah, yeah, Adrenaline bad boy, live and in the flesh.

I grabbed my phone and took a picture of them before shoving it back into my pocket. "I'm almost afraid to ask."

"Come on, lonely one," Drew winked. "Let's grab your shit. I'll give you a ride and we can figure out about getting your car later."

Jennifer sighed in relief. "I'm so glad you have friends here, Penelope. I'm so sorry! If you need a day or two to settle in—"

"I'm good and don't worry!" I smiled even though I still felt a bit sick to my stomach.

By the time Drew and I had grabbed my two suitcases and the pillow I'd brought with me, I was exhausted and ready to go to sleep.

"So where is this magical place you're taking me?" I asked in a tired voice.

Drew didn't answer, and five minutes later, we pulled up to the giant beach house I visited every afternoon.

"NO!" I shouted.

"Yes."

"Drew!"

"P-dog." He winked. "Come on, he already said yes. I texted him. What's the worst that could happen?" He leaned in and cupped my chin with his thumb and forefinger. "You stop being lonely? Get to know him better? He kisses you?"

I must have made a face because he jerked back and then clapped twice. And hit the steering wheel in amusement. "That dirty dog."

"Please don't say anything!"

"Oh, don't worry, I fully intend on telling the entire gang through our texting thread." He held out his phone. "But never fear, I'll just accuse him of it and then we'll all pester him for the next two hours while he thinks of ways to kill us all. It's a shit ton of fun."

"Guys are weird."

"We love the gossip." He opened up his door. "Let's do this."

I walked all the way up to the house like lead filled my legs, rolling my suitcases behind me. Meanwhile, Drew carried my pillow like he was on his way to his first sleepover, and when he knocked on the door he leaned against it like he was in some photo shoot and pulled Trevor in for a hug when he opened the door.

They broke apart.

Trevor looked ready to murder someone. Mainly Drew.

And Drew gave me a *"Don't worry, I got this"* look.

I had a very solid inkling he didn't *"have"* anything, but what could I even say?

"So…" Drew started backing away. "I think that's it. You kids have fun painting your toenails and braiding hair. If you need a third, you know where to find me, but I'm really only good at one thing at night. Isn't that right, Penelope? Or should I call you—"

"No more talking." I wagged my finger at him.

His face softened. I'd like to think he had the best intentions, just horrible execution when it came to doing good deeds.

"Thanks for being my date tonight," Drew said loud enough for the whole beach to hear him, and then he pulled me in for a hug and kissed my forehead, his lips slid down my cheek, and his whisper made me almost collapse against him. "Take it easy on him, baby steps."

I nodded.

And then he was gone, and I was staring up into Trevor's angry gaze, wondering if he would even let me into the house.

I wasn't sure how long we stayed like that.

But Bella broke the silence by moving around him and running toward me. "I knew it, I just knew it!"

"Knew what, sweetie?" I picked her up and twirled her around before drawing her close and kissing her nose.

"That you were gonna be my new mommy."

I almost dropped her.

Trevor's eyes got so wide it looked like his head was ready to explode.

"Oh, sweetie, no, that's not…" *Any time, Trevor, any time would be good, now would be good.* "There's a problem with my house, so your daddy is letting me stay in the guest room for the next week."

Her face fell, and then she lit up and whispered in my ear. "That's okay, I'll just keep wishing on the stars. After all…Daddy says every star eventually falls sooner or later."

Tears filled my eyes as I nodded and said, "Your daddy's right."

Chapter Fourteen

Trevor

I was going to murder Drew.

But first, I had to rein in the complete devastation caused by Bella's words. She needed a mom so bad, and I hated that there was a role that I as a father couldn't fill, a hole she had that no matter how many times I tried, seemed to always exist.

My chest felt tight, and the reheated pizza only made my stomach feel like a rock had settled on the bottom.

"Bella." I said her name softly. "Shouldn't you be in bed?"

"Yeah, but I heard Uncle Drew." Her little face was beaming like a lighthouse on a dark night.

"You and the rest of Seaside," I said in a voice that severely lacked any amusement on my part. The breeze picked up, carrying Penny's hair with it. Damn, she was pretty. It was like the more I got to know her, the prettier she became. What the hell was I going to do tomorrow morning? By the end of the week, I was going to need to walk around with my eyes closed and just pray I made it out the door alive. I let out a sigh. "Run up to your bed, and I'll read you a story in a few minutes, all right?"

"Can Penny read it?" Bella piped up, her eyes wide and excited at the opportunity to have someone other than her boring dad read to her. Fantastic. Maybe that was where my irritation was coming from. Penny wasn't staying, this wasn't a permanent thing. Sure, she would probably still help out if I asked, but I'd originally told her only until school started.

How could I change that from a few weeks to forever?

I was about to say no, mainly because I didn't want my daughter getting so attached that it broke her heart when Penny no longer read her stories, but she was clinging so tightly to Penny's neck, her little arms wrapped around it like a vise. And I realized that in another time, another life maybe, I would have been content to do the very same thing. "Yeah, baby, she can read it."

"Good! Thanks, Daddy. Come on, Penny!"

Penelope's eyes darted to me and then back to Bella before she flashed a wide smile that hit me like a punch to the gut. "Let's do it."

I held my breath when she walked by because I knew if I didn't, I'd get a whiff of intoxicating perfume with a hint of almond, and I'd do something stupid like kiss her again. Or maybe tell her that Drew was heavily medicated at all times and belonged in a mental hospital and that he peed the bed at night. He might never forgive me.

A smile tugged at my lips. I could live with that.

My chest felt tight as I watched them walk up the stairs, and then I leaned against the doorframe. Her bags were outside the door staring up at me, waiting for me to take them in, and all I kept thinking was that one day, those bags would be leaving, this wasn't permanent. This was just…life.

And life had been kicking me in the ass.

One day those bags would leave.

One day Penny would leave.

Where did that leave us when she was gone?

It wasn't supposed to be this hard.

She was supposed to be helping, not hindering, not making me feel things I hadn't felt in…

I frowned out at the distance, the salty air hanging heavy around me like the universe was waiting for my honesty, for my truth.

I hadn't felt that way about a woman in a long time.

And if I was being completely honest, I'd stayed with Jo because she was my children's mom. I hadn't slept with her in who knew how long? Separate bedrooms, separate lives. For the last two years at least.

A cold sweat broke out on my forehead as I grabbed Penny's bags and brought them into the house then up the stairs to the mother-in-law suite.

I walked by Eric's room then Malcom's. Both of them were sleeping, limbs hanging off the side of the bed ready to fall onto the floor in minutes. They were rowdy sleepers, which is why I didn't typically let them in my bed, too many black eyes to count when they were three years old.

"Goodnight Moon…" Penny finished, then kissed Bella on the top of her head while I saw movement in Eric's room.

How was it humanly possible to be sleeping that hard one minute, then snickering the next? Unbelievable.

"Boys. Bed!" I yelled.

"Sorry, Dad," they muttered together like they were anything but sorry. Maybe I should let them share a room? I always thought that space was the way to go, but more and more Malcom was sneaking into Eric's room and asking to stay.

I let out a frustrated breath and glanced back into my daughter's room as Penny pulled the covers up to Bella's chin and then gave her another kiss on the forehead.

Pain squeezed my chest so tightly, so effectively and efficiently that I had to look away.

Penny shut the door with a quiet click and faced me.

I wanted to torture myself with information about their date, even though I was pretty sure I knew exactly how good it had been for Drew.

Bastard.

"Drink?" I asked, apparently needing alcohol to have that sort of conversation with her.

Why him?

I mean, he was good looking, charismatic—okay, I needed to not go down that dark, depressing road. He was free. I wasn't. Maybe deep down that was what she craved, to be someone's world.

Kinda hard to compete with that when I already had three running circles around me on a daily basis.

"Yeah." She frowned and then nodded toward the kitchen. "That actually sounds great. I'm not a huge beer drinker, though Drew tried to—"

"Convince you?" I bet he did. Why did she have to catch Drew's eye? Him of all people? Really?

"It was okay but not my favorite. He kept ordering different kinds until I made him stop."

I smirked. "He likes it when people like what he likes, mainly because he's an expert when it comes to himself. Narcissist and all that."

Penny scrunched up her nose and smiled. "Isn't everyone like that, though? I mean narcissism aside, it's nice to have similar interests."

We couldn't be any more different if we tried. "Yeah I guess so. Which means if you don't like gin and tonic..." I tried to lighten the mood.

"Ahhhh, with lime?"

"Always." I winked and grabbed two glasses, then looked around for the limes only to find Penny already slicing them open for us.

The woman was perfect.

Damn it.

I was killing Drew later.

And shoving my drumsticks up his ass.

Alcohol.

I grabbed the bottle of Beefeater Gin and poured a generous amount in both cups, then grabbed ice while Penny grabbed the tonic water and started to pour.

It was too damn easy with her, like she belonged in my house, my kitchen. Like making her a permanent fixture in my life wasn't just a dream but destiny.

I held up my glass, she held up hers. "Cheers."

She smiled and clinked hers against mine then took a long, slow sip that had me staring for an embarrassing amount of time at her neck and the way the liquid flowed down her perfect throat.

Great, now I was obsessed with her throat.

When had this happened?

Seeing her with Drew had made me want to snap.

Seeing him flirting with her made me want to commit a crime, and now I was drinking with three kids sleeping upstairs, all because I couldn't calm my racing pulse. And if I was being really honest, I knew if I didn't have something to hold in my hands, I'd reach for her.

And I wasn't sure anymore if that was what she wanted, not since the date. Besides, how did I even begin to explain that to the kids? I kiss her, I like her, yet she also works for us, but no, she's not your mother...

"So." I cleared my throat and leaned against the countertop.

"How'd the date go?"

Penny smiled over her glass. "Probing a bit?"

"A lot, not a bit." I laughed and took another fortifying swallow.

"We decided we would be great friends."

"Joint decision?" I frowned as the alcohol got stuck in my throat and left a lingering burn.

"After some explaining, yes." She nodded slowly. "Though it's Drew, so I'm sure reminding him what friendship means will be a daily necessity."

I barked out another laugh. "Yeah, good luck with that. When he sees something he wants…" I shrugged.

"What about you?"

That got my attention, and I jerked my head up and snorted. "Drew doesn't want me like that, thank God."

Her eyes narrowed, she put down her drink and leaned over the counter. Her shirt was just low enough for me to see breasts; two perfect mounds that I wanted to cup, to kiss and suck and squeeze and…shit, what were we talking about again? "Not Drew, I'm talking about when you want something…do you just blindly pursue?"

"Used to." I gritted my teeth. "But that's what I did with my ex, and look how that turned out." I exhaled roughly, the final reminder released into the universe. I had been impulsive with her, impulsive with my heart, ready to just toss it at the first woman who I thought truly got me. And I was wrong, so very wrong. "Besides, I have three other people to think about, even if I wanted…" My voice fell as sadness flashed across her face. "You know what I mean. It's not just me anymore. I have to think about them, what's best for them, what's best for us."

"That's what I thought," she said softly, looking away and finishing her drink like a champ. "Just so you know…" I watched her move around my kitchen like it was hers. "Your kids aren't holding you back. At least from this position, the one I'm standing in, they seem to be the driving force behind everything you do."

The truth of it slammed into me. "Twenty-year-old me could make mistakes, and it was only about me. Thirty-one-year-old me has baggage that comes with him. Thirty-one-year-old me sees it reflected in my kids' eyes. I get what you're saying, they're the driving force but also the reason I can't—"

"Right," she finished. "Okay." Another nod as she started to walk away.

I grabbed her by the wrist and pulled her against me.

Her eyes locked onto mine. "Is this where you tell me it's not me, it's you?"

"This is where I tell you I wish I had met you in a different life."

"Funny." She pulled away from me. "Since I was just thinking how lucky I am to meet you in this one."

Disappointment filled the room.

Questions asked.

Answers given.

Choices made.

And I had to wonder what would have happened had I told her the only thing I've been wanting to pursue for the last week and a half? Had been her heart.

Chapter Fifteen

Penelope

I slept like crap.

And it wasn't the drink that did it.

Nope, all signs pointed to the amazing guy that refused to let me in. Not that I'd asked, but I'd at least been wondering if we could go in that direction. I mean, we'd held hands, kissed. Oh God, now I sounded like a stupid teenager with her first crush.

The point, I thought as I got out of bed that morning and put on my clothes to head into work, was that there were feelings. Big time feelings. And he'd looked pissed about Drew, but that was it.

No, hey we kissed let's talk about it.

No, hey so I like holding hands but I swear it's not a hand fetish.

It's a you fetish.

Let's get married and make sweet love and fill this house with our offspring!

Okay, so he wasn't going to say that, but he could at least say that there was something—anything.

I mean, there was something there. I felt the way he looked at me, the way I looked at him, that kiss. I almost started fanning myself—people don't just kiss people they hate. At least in my world. You kiss them because you want them, because you're attracted, because something exists in time and space between two human bodies, two souls, that must be recognized.

And although he kind of acknowledged it, I had been shut down so fast that my head spun.

The more I thought about it, the angrier I became, until I realized I was stomping down the stairs into the living room.

I quieted my steps and walked by the couch, only to stop and frown down at it.

Trevor was sleeping.

Remote in hand.

TV on.

And because the universe hates me, he chose that moment to open his eyes and stare up at me then fall to the floor. "Son of a bitch, you scared the shit out of me."

I covered my face with my hands. "I'm sorry, I was just walking by and trying to figure out why you were sleeping on the couch and—"

"I didn't want to miss you." He rubbed sleep from his eyes. "I was supposed to give you a car or a ride, remember, since Drew dropped you off?"

"Well, yeah, but—"

His eyes darkened. "Please tell me your plan wasn't to walk two miles at five a.m., in the dark, with predators lurking?"

I smiled. "There are no predators lurking, especially in a place that doesn't even have Uber!" Predators. He was adorable. Wait, no, stop.

He snorted. "You're taking the Jeep, give me your keys and I'll have Drew grab your car later. It's the least he can do."

"Jeep?" I tried not to sound too excited as he shot me a pointed glance over his shoulder then walked over to the counter and handed me the keys.

"Try not to crash it."

"Thanks, Dad." I grinned.

He glowered. "Not funny."

"Wasn't trying to be funny." I folded my arms and gave him a challenging glare.

He pressed his hands down on my shoulders and then pulled me against him. My arms dropped to my sides. "I don't know what I'm doing."

"Does anyone in life?"

"I want—"

"Daddy!" Malcom made his way into the kitchen rubbing his eyes.

"Can I watch a movie?"

"Sleep, I just want sleep," he muttered under his breath. "No, buddy, you have to go to bed."

"I'm scared."

"Sleep with your brother."

Malcom's bottom lip trembled a bit.

"Hey!" I intervened. I hated his tears. "Why don't you go sleep in my room a bit? I left the fireplace on, and my favorite bear's in the bed guarding my things!"

"You sleep with a bear?"

"It protects me." I winked. "I mean, you don't have to, but there is a TV in there. Maybe after you sleep a few hours, Dad will let you watch?"

"Yay! Dad, can I?"

"Yeah." He kissed the top of his head "Off you go."

Malcom ran full speed toward my bedroom, and part of me felt sad that I couldn't stay home and cuddle with him while watching Sesame Street.

His little hands and feet would be under the covers, limbs taking over the entire bed. Malcom slept like he was trying to use as much space as possible.

My heart ached.

Trevor shook his head in what looked like frustration. "I need to do something about their sleeping arrangements. Kid's not sleeping. He keeps trying to sneak into Eric's room."

"So let him," I piped up in a strong voice. "They're twins, and Malcom needs comfort. Honestly, putting them together might help Eric just as much as Malcolm. He's hurting too. He just lashes out, whereas Malcom…"

"Malcom has a tender heart." Trevor took the words right out of my mouth.

"Tender but still strong, just like his dad," I said softly.

Trevor reached for me.

I stumbled back. "Okay, so I'll just be heading to the garage now."

"Running away?" he taunted, looking deliciously sexy in no shirt and a low pair of track pants that hugged his hips.

I dangled the keys in the air. "I'll try not to get a ticket."

"If you get a ticket in Seaside, I'll be more impressed than pissed."

I flashed him a wide smile. "Thanks for this."

"Thanks for..." He stopped and then whispered, "...everything."

My throat clogged up a bit as I nodded, not trusting myself to speak without confessing how much I was falling for him and his family, and I quickly made my way to the garage and the waiting Jeep.

He had brought three cars with him.

I was taking one.

And I was going to pretend it was normal.

This was normal.

Employer.

Employee.

I clicked the key fob to unlock the doors and let out a little gasp when I saw the caramel colored lush leather seats.

It was normal to moan when getting into your employer's car, um...right?

I sighed and gripped the steering wheel just as the garage door went up. Trevor stood next to the door, waving me off.

His friggin' eight pack flexed for the world to see.

Yup. Normal.

I turned on the SUV and drove out of his million dollar beach house toward my job, with fresh tracks of his voice playing in the background. And his abs in my rearview mirror.

So normal it was almost scary, right?

Chapter Sixteen

Trevor

"Daaaaaaad," Eric yelled as he bounded down the stairs. "Can I play some video games?"

I was well on my fourth cup of coffee.

It was about an hour until Penny was supposed to show up.

And I felt like shit.

Worse than shit.

And as much as I wanted to blame it on the fact that I'd confused Penny and was mentally exhausted—I knew it was worse than that.

I was getting sick.

I never got sick.

My hands were clammy as I lifted the mug to my lips and sipped, then I grimaced and nodded. "Yeah, buddy."

The next hour went by painfully slow, partially because I missed her even though I shouldn't, and partially because the more seconds that passed the sicker I got, to the point that I finally lay on the couch next to Eric and told Malcom to keep an eye on Bella.

My throat burned, and my body ached. I turned on my side, and the next thing I knew tiny hands were shaking me awake. "Is he dead?"

"Let's hope not," Penny said with amusement in her voice. "Why don't you guys go upstairs and wash your hands, and I'll take you all out for lunch. How does that sound?"

"Hooray!" They all let out little screams of excitement as if they'd been prisoners in their own home. I would have rolled my eyes had I had the energy.

Cold fingertips pressed against my forehead. "Trevor?"

"Penny." I rasped her name. Damn she was pretty and I wasn't even staring at her. I could feel her though, feel her beauty through her skin. Wait, was that even possible? "Penny?"

"I'm here." Something cold and wet hit my forehead. "I think you have a fever. I'm going to get you some Tylenol to bring it down, okay?"

"So hot," I grumbled and then gripped her wrist. "You feel cold."

"Because you're sick," she said softly. "I'm sorry I'm late. It was busy at the coffee shop, something about Adrenaline doing a free concert."

I snorted out a laugh. "We need music to do that."

"Well, you could use your old stuff, though I'm not sure how the rumor got started."

"You and Drew." I might be delirious, but even I knew how easy it was to assume things, like the fact that she was out with Drew the night before and worked at a coffee shop that often had free mic night. "People like to draw conclusions. People are stupid, like his ego could even fit in that shit hole."

"Excuse me?"

My eyes surged open, temples pounding, "Penny, no, not—that's not what I—"

"You think I work in a shit hole?" She stood and crossed her arms.

No, I needed her to sit back down.

To touch me with her fingertips.

To talk to me and make me feel better.

"I'm sick, I'm not thinking clearly." I knew I was already screwed by the hurt expression on her face. "Penny, please."

"No," she whispered, tears in her eyes. "You're right, it's better this way, better to know how you really feel. I'm the hired help, and I work in a shit hole." Her smile was sad. "Kids, you ready?"

"Penny, just wait—" I tried to sit up but my skull felt like it was on fire, and I winced and fell back.

"I'm going to text your egotistical friend and let him know you can't make it to the studio this afternoon, then I'm going to let your bandmates know that they need to pay their final respects."

"I'm sick, not dying."

She glared. "We'll. See."

"You plan on killing me for insulting you?"

"If the fever doesn't get you then yes, it's a huge possibility. You don't have to be an asshole just because you're sick, and just because you're loaded doesn't mean you get to make fun of where I work, got it?"

"I think the neighbors even got it, could you please keep your voice down?" I saw three of her. Still beautiful, even as triplets. "Penny? Would you look at me?"

"No. I'm pissed at you!"

"Dad, what's pissed mean?" Malcom bounded down the stairs followed by Bella and Eric, each of them looking at me expectantly. I groaned and pulled a throw-pillow over my head.

"Who wants McDonald's?" She clapped her hands. Loudly. The next thing I knew all of the kids were running out the door and she was sending me one last sad look over her shoulder.

Sleep overtook me again.

I dreamed of her smile.

And then we were kissing, my tongue was in her mouth, and it was perfect. I pressed her against the fridge, things tumbled inside, I picked her up by the hips and mauled her, not realizing how soft her hair was or her skin. It was everything I wanted and knew I couldn't have.

"Is that for me?" Drew's voice jolted me out of my slumber. I blinked up to see him hovering over me with a giant grin on his face and his phone pointed down south. "Because I feel like that breaks at least ten rules of friendship."

"Huh?"

He pointed.

I covered myself with the throw pillow. My head was still pounding, and the sound of tiny feet running around the house was nowhere to be found.

I hated it.

Just like I hated the fact that Penny had left pissed off.

And now I was having arousing dreams about the off-limits nanny. Perfect.

"I'm sick. Go away." I waved him off.

Instead, just like the plague, he stayed and plopped himself down on the couch across from me. "So your girl sounded upset when she called."

"She was supposed to text," I grumbled, rubbing my temples with my fingertips. "Could we not do this right now?"

"How's she taste?"

"The hell?" I looked up. "One more word and I'm going to impale you with my drumsticks."

"Ouch." He grinned and spread his arms wide. "Where would our band be without me?"

"At this point, I don't really care." I lay back down and kicked him with both feet.

"Someone's upset." He sighed. "Look, the guys went to the studio, laid down some really good tracks, and worked on the two we were messing with yesterday. Career-wise we're on top of things, you're on top of things, but personally..."

I groaned. "Personally, what?"

"You're a mess."

"Why are you here again?"

"Pretty Penelope said if she came back and saw you sleeping she might suffocate you and she didn't want to go to prison for murder. I'm here to save your life. You're welcome."

A few beats of silence went by before I admitted, "I accidentally called the coffee shop she works at a shit hole."

Drew burst out laughing. "You're an idiot."

"I'm delirious and exhausted, I have a fever, big difference," I pointed out as I blindly reached for the glass of water that had been left on the coffee table, probably by Penny. Even in her anger, she was taking care of me.

Damn it!

"You gotta make it up to her."

"How am I supposed to do that?"

"Hell if I know. I've never been in a committed relationship. The only girl I ever got close to is currently marrying one of our lead singers, so...."

"Right." We never talked about his past.

The animosity between Drew and Will still existed like this disease that refused to fully leave the body, so we left it alone. At least they got along and could be friends again, as long as they didn't talk about it.

The drugs, the partying, the cheating.

We kept it all under the rug where it belonged.

Where, frankly, Drew protected it like a baby.

He said if he let it out, it made it real.

And he wasn't sure he could handle his own truth.

I didn't blame him.

I could barely tolerate mine.

"Am I an asshole?" I asked, probably the wrong person, but whatever.

"Not always," he said with a shrug. "I would say you're the least assholey of all of us. How's that make you feel?"

"Honestly, not well." I groaned into my hands. "Because you're a dick."

"Thanks, man." Drew released a sinister laugh. "Look, she's with the kids. In fact, they've been gone three hours, they went to Mc Donald's then the aquarium. If you ask me, she deserves more money than whatever you're paying her, plus her place is completely ruined. I stopped by today, and she isn't moving back in, not for a long ass time." He was quiet and then, "You're loaded. What could you possibly do that would make this situation better for her? Easier?"

"Uhhhhhh..." My mind drew a blank, but then I suggested, "Buy her a house?"

"Sometimes I wonder why they call you the mature one," Drew muttered. "No, dumbass, but you could treat her. Flowers aren't something girls buy for themselves. Hell, you could even give her a raise and demand she go shopping, make her feel special, that's all I'm saying."

"I do not know how to do that as her friend," I admitted. "Not after tasting her—"

"*Then*—" he interrupted pointedly "—you better figure it out, and soon, because she's going to be back in about five minutes."

"Shit."

"Good luck!" He jumped to his feet and walked to the door. "For what it's worth, I never stood a chance."

"What the hell are you talking about?" I frowned in his direction.

"She likes you, man." He sobered. "Hell if I know why she prefers a single dad with three messy kids over this." He gestured along the length of his body with a laugh. "But she does, so the least you can do is figure your shit out and fast."

The door slammed behind him.

I stared into the silence.

Hating it even more.

I wanted loud.

I wanted my kids.

I wanted Penny in my kitchen.

I wanted what I was terrified to have.

And I was petrified that if I touched her more, I'd ruin what shaky ground we were already on.

I had kids to think about.

Drew didn't.

I quickly ran upstairs and tried to freshen up a bit. I looked like hell, but I only had enough energy to put on a fresh shirt, brush my teeth, and make it back downstairs.

And just as Drew had promised, minutes later the kids came bounding into the house in a mixture of coats flying, shoes getting pulled off, shoving, and then yelling about dibs on the video games.

Penny rounded the corner with a tired smile on her face.

"Massage," I blurted.

She stilled. "You've got to be kidding me!" She threw her hands in the air. The kids ran past her up the stairs. Each of them had a bag. She must have taken them to a store too. "My feet ache, you kiss me then tell me nothing can happen, basically push me toward your bandmate, then let me stay with you, almost kiss me again, tell me no, insult my work, and now you want me to massage you?"

"You done yet?" I grinned.

She glared.

"I meant massage *for* you. You need a massage, and since I'm feeling a little bit better, I figured I could at least, you know…" I gulped.

She gaped and then nodded slowly, her cheeks pinking. "Yeah, um, let me just get the kids down for a nap and…" She begrudgingly muttered sorry under her breath and walked past me, then tripped on the first stair.

"You all right?"

"Yup!" She ran up the rest of them and minutes later returned with a bottle of lotion and handed it to me.

"Ah, getting fancy on me?" I teased.

"Are you really feeling better?" she countered.

I sat up and shrugged. Honestly, no. My head was pounding and I still felt delirious, but I couldn't decipher if it was because I was going to touch her again or if I was still sick.

"Sit down." I decided not to answer her.

"Where?" She put her hands on her hips.

"Right here." I pointed to the space on the floor right in front of my legs and then opened them a bit. Maybe this was a bad idea, the touching.

She quickly moved to the floor and sat between my legs. My knees were next to her head and all I kept thinking was that it would be so easy to tug her up against me, to kiss the back of her neck and grip her ass with both hands.

Focus.

Her hair was already in a ponytail, which for some reason made me sad. I wanted to touch it, to move it out of the way, to feel its weight in my hand.

I cleared my throat and started massaging her shoulders.

She hung her head forward. "That feels amazing."

Yeah, it did.

I was supposed to be doing something for her and already it was doing something for me, to me.

I stopped and grabbed some lotion then spread it across her neck, careful not to get it on her shirt. I massaged deep and ran my hands down her bare shoulders. A flimsy strap stood in the way of full skin-on-skin contact.

I hated that strap more than I hated Drew, and that was saying a lot.

She moaned and then her head fell back against my lap. I kept rubbing her neck then moved upwards, until I got to her face, my knuckles grazing her jaw.

Her eyelashes fluttered open. "What are we doing?"

"You're sitting. I'm massaging."

"Right." She looked like she didn't believe me.

The yearning was too much. Maybe the sickness made me weak. Maybe I'd just been weak all along.

"I'm sorry." I licked my lips. "For what I said."

"I'm sorry for yelling at you." She stared up at me, her head resting in my lap, my hands touching her.

Tense silence descended.

And so did my head.

Lower, lower, until I captured her lips in a punishing kiss. She wrapped her arms back around my head as I deepened the kiss.

She broke away from me, turned, and crawled into my lap.

This. This was what I wanted.

What I needed.

I groaned against her mouth. "I'm better at this when I'm not sick and running a fever."

"I..." She kissed down my neck. "Believe..." She nipped my lower lip. "You."

"God, you taste good."

"You said—"

"Forget what I said," I whispered against her mouth. "Just don't make me stop kissing you. I don't think I could handle it."

"Well, you are sick...."

"Yes, feel sorry for me, kiss it better." I grinned as I angled my head to get more of her taste.

"I'll try" was her response.

And try she fucking did.

Chapter Seventeen

Penelope

I was crossing so many lines.

Lines that felt good.

His skin beneath my hands felt rough, like he hadn't shaved in two days, and the friction against my mouth was painful and passionate. With each movement, I was trying to get closer and closer to him.

"You're sick," I whispered against his mouth as the clock in the living room ticked slowly like we needed a reminder that there were kids upstairs, that we both had very different lives as he'd so painfully reminded me earlier that day.

Attraction was one thing.

Acting on it was another.

But believing it could go past those two things? That just seemed like the road to a broken heart.

"Hey." He braced my head with both of his hands. "I have a headache, and yeah, I feel like shit, but it's not like I have a head cold or anything."

"Because those are worse?"

"Always." He grinned. "Penny…" He swept me up in another kiss that had me forgetting I was straddling him on his couch with his kids upstairs.

"Daaaaaaaad!" Eric wailed. "Malcom hit me!"

"Hit him back," he grumbled against my lips before pulling away and yelling up the stairs. "Kinda busy right now!"

"Daaaaaaaaad!" Footsteps thumped overhead, heading toward the stairs.

Slowly, I pried myself away from Trevor's warm body, from the muscles that held me close and the lips that kept me there. On wobbly legs, I moved around the couch and walked into the kitchen while Eric made a beeline for his dad and threw his hands in the air in frustration.

Trevor got on his level. "You guys need to stop fighting."

Malcom ran down the stairs yelling, "He said Mom isn't ever coming back! Tell him, Dad, tell him it's not true!"

Bella stood at the top of the stairway, tears in her eyes.

I wanted to fix it. God, how did I fix it?

I hated that Trevor was right. They were his number one priority. It would be selfish of me to ask for more, to ask for him to make space for one more when they were barely surviving.

"Bella, sweet." I beamed up at her. "Do you want to help me make some cookies?"

Eric's head whipped in my direction. "What kind?"

"Depends." I crossed my arms. "Are you going to be nice to your brother?"

He seemed to think about it while Malcom wiped the tears on his cheeks.

"Tell you what. I'll let all three of you help while your dad rests." I gave Trevor a pointed look. "And while they're baking, we can pick out a board game."

"Yay!" Bella cheered.

Both boys shrugged, but I could see the excitement glimmer in their eyes. They were good kids, they were just hurting, and hurting people hurt people, didn't they?

"Eric," Trevor intervened. "Apologize to Malcom, please."

Eric turned to his brother and sighed like the world was against him, his shoulders slumped forward. "Sorry I said Mom wasn't coming back."

"It's okay." Malcom sniffled. "Don't you want her to, Eric?"

"No." Eric said in an indifferent voice. "She used to make us be quiet and sit in front of the TV while she invited her friends over. She never played with us like Dad or Penny."

I sucked in a sharp breath.

"She's not good enough for us," Eric added in a confident voice as he made his way into the kitchen and stared me down. "We need directions."

And that was it.

I sent Trevor back to the couch and played with the kids. By the time we were done with the cookies, cleanup, and the board game, it was dinnertime. Trevor had fallen asleep at some point.

I ordered pizza.

He slept through it all, so hard in fact, that I walked by several times to make sure he was still breathing. The guy was exhausted, and I wondered if it had more to do with him being a single dad trying to do it all than the fact that he was feeling sick.

The guy probably hadn't truly slept in years.

I pulled a blanket up over his body and gave a jolt when Bella appeared in front of me. "Are you going to marry my daddy?"

"Uhhhh." I kept my voice low and smiled down at her. "Honey, your daddy's wonderful, but we aren't getting married."

"Oh." Her brows furrowed. "But you like him, right?"

"Of course," I said slowly. "But your daddy and I are just friends."

"Ohhhhh." She nodded. "Does that mean I can kiss friends at school like you did Daddy today?"

I gaped. "No, no, no, no, you see your daddy was…not feeling well and kisses make people feel better but only when you're…sixteen."

Trevor grunted in his sleep.

"Or thirty-five. Yes, that was my…first kiss, and even then, I'm clearly not old enough to be doing that. I'm sorry." I lied through my teeth. I was only 27 and had my first kiss at fifteen.

Yup, I was apologizing to an almost four-year-old.

Great.

Perfect.

"I guess that makes more sense." She beamed up at me. "You're not leaving us, are you?"

"No, why would you think that?"

"People leave." She looked down at her feet.

"I'm not most people." I pulled her in for a hug. "Now go brush your teeth and get your PJs on, and I'll be up in a bit to tuck you in."

"Can we sing Twinkles?"

"At least four times!" I winked. "Maybe five, if the guys join in with instruments that don't resemble farts."

"Boys are gross."

"That's why we don't kiss them," I added, scrunching up my nose.

She wrapped her arms around my neck and whispered, "But Daddy isn't gross. Maybe I'll marry him one day?"

"Maybe." I kissed her forehead. "I'll be up in a few minutes."

She scampered off and raced up the stairs.

"You're so good with her." Trevor's voice was thick with sleep as his eyes opened and stared right through me to the center of my existence. I was sucked into his universe, into his vortex, and there was no escaping, was there? "Thanks for making her wait until thirty-five. Guess I should be more careful."

"We need to be more than careful. We can't…" I sighed. "That can't happen again."

"It can." He moved to his feet so fast I stumbled backwards. "It will."

"So sure of yourself?" I teased, my body already pulsing in anticipation.

"Absolutely." He didn't look away from me. Instead, he stood, leaned close, and pulled me into his embrace, then left me as he slowly walked up the stairs. "I'll put the kids to bed. Why don't you go take a bath and relax?"

"I don't have a tub in my bathroom." I frowned at his retreating form.

He looked over his shoulder and gave me the sexiest smile ever. "I know. But I do."

"Trevor—"

"You know where it's at."

"I don't think—"

"Don't think," he interrupted again once he made it to the top of the stairwell. "And if you're being really adventurous, you can use the princess bubble bath. Bella swears by it."

How could I say no to his smile?

To the princess bubble bath?

To the heated looks he gave me?

"Okay," I said, whispering my answer like a coward.

Chapter Eighteen

Trevor

Bella made me sing Twinkle Twinkle at least a dozen times before she finally fell asleep, still holding her mom's black T-shirt like it was her teddy bear. Irrational anger coursed through me.

Because how dare she.

How. Dare. She.

It played on repeat over and over again in my head until I was sick with it, and when I walked by Malcom's room and noticed that he was already crawling out of bed, I crooked my finger toward him. "Let's go, buddy, you're sleeping in Eric's room tonight."

He froze and then, "Really?"

"Yup. We're going to try to keep the smell minimal, and the only way to do that with you two boys is to keep you in the same small, controlled environment."

Malcom sniffed under his arms. "I smell like Batman Blueberry Wash, Dad."

"Now." I grinned. "Just wait until tomorrow morning when it smells like a rat straight up sacrificed its entire family on the altar of your underwear."

He let out a giggle. "Rat farts."

"I asked for that one, didn't I?"

"Yeah, Dad, you're funny." He sprinted past me and into his brother's room. "Eric! I get to sleep on the bottom bunk!"

I leaned against the doorframe and stared at Eric's thunderous expression and then almost laughed when he tossed a pillow toward Malcom's face and said in an authoritative voice, "You better not fart."

Ah, boys.

"Bed." I tried my most commanding voice and pointed at both of them. As if a parent's pointer finger was the one thing they couldn't look away from, they both gave me wide eyes and nods, with unison "Yes, Dad's."

Finally.

I closed their door and slowly walked toward the master suite. One of the reasons I'd blindly chosen the beach house was because the master suite had a beautiful view of the ocean, was close to the studio, and had a fireplace in the bathroom with heated tile floors. It wasn't as nice as my place in Malibu, but it felt more like home than that mansion ever had.

I opened the door to the master and shut it quietly behind me as the sound of the bath water running filled the air almost like an electrical charge.

The fireplace was running.

The curtains were pulled back, and HGTV was on in the background, though the flat screen TV hanging over the fireplace was at least turned down to almost silent.

I would have hated for anything to drown out the water.

Or the fact that she was either in it or about to get in it.

The smell of Bella's bubble bath assaulted me as I made my way into the large marble bathroom with its custom crown molding and large bay windows and was stunned stupid.

Penny was lounging in the bathtub, her toes up on the edges. Her nails were pink, and I fixated on them like a man who'd never seen feet before.

But they were so feminine, so…normal.

Penny had the ability to make me feel both normal and like I could do anything in the world.

It was addicting, the way she smiled at me, the way she silently encouraged me even when she didn't realize she was doing it. Damn, the woman communicated with her eyes just as well as she did with her words.

I wanted her story.

I needed it.

"Champagne?" I asked with a tilt of my head.

"Please." She sucked on her bottom lip and then tugged it up with her teeth while I moved to the opposite end of the bathroom where the wet bar was located. I pulled a chilled bottle and two glasses and brought everything to the edge of the marble tub.

She was still staring at me.

And I was trying like hell not to burn a hole through all the bubbles that hid what I knew would be my favorite parts of her.

"So…" I grabbed a nearby towel and covered the cork, then quickly popped it off the champagne. "Are you feeling relaxed?"

"Relaxed and guilty." She sighed as I handed her the champagne. "Aren't you the sick one?"

"I'm feeling—" A bubble floated by her right breast, exposing more skin. "—fantastic suddenly."

"Maybe you just needed the sleep?" She lifted the flute to her lips.

"Or maybe I just needed you," I said honestly.

We locked eyes.

"You have to mean it," she said in a quiet but stern voice. "I'm not…" She sighed. "I'm not like other women. I'm not from LA, I don't do one night stands, and I truly don't think my heart could take it if you said yes only to whisper no the very next day."

"I wouldn't do that to you." I wanted to tell her that it was almost offensive she would think so, but I knew what my past looked like when I was a teen, I knew what people thought of celebrities with too much fame and money. "You don't have to be afraid that I'm going to see you naked, kiss my way down your skin, then suddenly decide I don't want more."

Her lips parted. "I came here for a fresh start, you know."

I pulled my shirt over my head. "Oh yeah? So far so good, then?"

She smirked. "Stop trying to distract me."

I dipped my fingers into the tub, flicking bubbles in her direction. "I bet this isn't what you had in mind when you moved here, hmm?"

She laughed. "More like…new scenery."

I dropped my jeans just as she took a sip of champagne and choked.

"You all right?" I grinned.

"Yeah," she croaked. "Perfect. Great scenery."

I barked out a laugh. "Yeah, that's what I was going for."

Her eyes raked over me like she was giddy to get to know every inch of my body better.

I was done waiting.

I still tasted her.

I still felt her even though she was all wet and about to get wetter.

I pulled my boxer briefs down and then very slowly crawled into the huge tub.

She gaped like she'd never seen an aroused man before and then blushed like she was afraid I was going to pounce on her.

Not far from the truth.

Our legs slid against one another's.

I let out a little moan when she reached for my foot and started massaging. "So you like baths?"

"If they all start like this and end with you in my bed, yeah, I fucking love baths."

She dropped my foot. "Now I feel like you were faking your sickness."

"Now I feel like I need to thank you for taking care of the kids, for being there for me, for being...unapologetically you." I moved toward her, the water sloshing over the sides. I set her flute down on the side and covered her body with mine, my legs straddling her hips as I leaned in and stole a kiss, followed by another, and another, until she wrapped her arms around my neck and held on while our bodies slid against one another, bubbles moving away from the small waves, and then I was moving my right hand down her chest.

"Made for my hands, aren't they?" I said gruffly against her mouth as I weighed her breasts in my hands then moved back so I could get a better look, so I could memorize the way her nipples seemed to strain toward me. Mouth swollen, she waited with a hooded expression.

"You all right?" I smiled as she gave her head a shake like she was under my spell.

"No," she said, shocking me, and then she licked her lips as she grabbed my hands and pressed them back against her breasts. "I think I need more attention, here, here..." She moved my hands down her body. "And definitely down there..."

"So much for trying to go slow and be a gentleman." I gripped her by the hips and slid my fingertips down her thigh.

"You don't have to be, not right now, not with me. I just want you to be you."

I smiled against her lips. "Just remember you asked for this."

"For wha—"

I swallowed her shriek of pleasure as my fingers found her core, stretching her, flicking her sensitive flesh, demanding she come apart against me.

"This." I went deeper, softer, faster, slower. I pulled out all the stops and changed with every inflection of her moan, with every tense movement of her body. When her head fell back and she collapsed back into the water, muscles relaxed, I knew I would never forget the look on her face, wet pieces of hair sticking to her neck, lips slightly parted, eyes closed.

Mine.

"I'm not letting you go." I kissed her with every ounce of passion I had, with relentless conviction that this was where my path had taken me, straight into this woman's arms. And I was suddenly thankful I'd gone through hell, because I'd finally discovered that heaven was real.

And it belonged to me.

"Come on." I held out my hand. "I'm not done with you yet, and the last thing we need is a flood in the bathroom."

"Flood?" She yawned.

"Are you seriously yawning right now?" I laughed, wrapping a towel around her as she stood.

"Sorry!" Her face flamed red. "It's not you, I just, I can't believe I just yawned. It was instinctual, you know like after you get the best orgasm of your life by a guy's *hand* and suddenly go wow I'm so relaxed I could just dream of a few fingers for the rest of my life and die happy."

Shit, my grin got more and more permanent the more she talked. "You're good for my ego, you know that?"

"You almost made up for the ketchup on your shirt that first day," she teased with a wink. "What's this flood busin—Oh." She stared down at the water then back up at me with wide eyes. "Was that from us?"

"You," I corrected. "Apparently you have trouble sitting still when someone's trying to bring you past the brink of sanity over and over again."

She covered her face with one hand and held her towel up with another.

I dried myself off, then ran her towel down her body and pried it from both of her hands.

She seemed uncertain.

"Are you on birth control?" I asked.

"Y-yes." She swayed toward me.

"I'm clean. Sadly I had to double check since some dick was dipping itself into my ex-wife, but know, I would never…put you at risk for anything. And the only reason I ask is because I'm a single dad who had no intentions of finding anyone like you. Ever. Not just in Seaside, but ever. I also haven't been with anyone, including the ex in years." Tears filled her eyes. "So I don't have condoms here. Besides, there's something very wrong about storing condoms next to the Legos."

She burst out laughing.

"What I'm saying…" I pulled her naked body into my arms. "…is this isn't a one-time thing, this isn't something I do. This means more, all right?"

A smile broke across Penny's face that made her glow, and she wrapped her arms around me. "And here every time I stared at your poster I imagined you as the guy who had a new girl every night."

"I knew you looked at my poster. It would make my day to know you circled my face with a heart and imagined what holding my hand would feel like." I lifted her into the air and set her down.

Penny laughed. "Sorry to say I didn't heart your face, but I did wonder…."

I waited.

And waited.

"Wonder?"

"Mmmm…" She crooked her finger. "Not when I was a teen, but last year, when you guys had your tour and were at the Grammys…"

Oh God, I knew where this was going.

I couldn't hide my smile if I tried.

"And you wore those leather pants." She slowly moved to her knees in front of my bed. "If all the rumors were true, that you have to literally tuck in order to perform in tight pants, plus those pictures went viral really fast."

"Some might say the hashtag bulge never had so much play." I laughed, already painfully aroused.

"Yup." She popped the P and lowered her eyes.

"Disappointed?"

"More like, how are you going to make sure you don't puncture a lung?" She gripped my length with her hand and moved.

My hips jerked toward her. "Yeah, you shouldn't do that to me if you don't want me to toss you against the bed. Swear it will be the best five seconds of your life."

She released me and burst out laughing. "This isn't how I thought it was going to be."

"So you thought about it?" I walked her backwards toward the bed.

"Yeah, just don't put that in your recommendation letter. *Nanny thought about Dad naked, often.*"

"Often, hmm?"

"Here." She handed me a pillow. "Just get it over with."

"I'm not smothering you with a pillow." I tossed it aside and lifted her onto the bed, my hands stilled on her hips. "Besides, I'm just as guilty. I knew I was fucked the minute I invited you into my house."

"It was the pot roast." She nodded her head seriously.

"It was your heart," I whispered, devouring her next words before she could utter them. "And your crazy beautiful smile." I pulled away and then kissed down her neck. "It was the way you treated my kids." I slammed my mouth against hers and positioned myself near her entrance. "It was you being you."

"Fresh start." Our eyes met, time stopped. It was just us alone in the universe making love.

Two people on separate paths, somehow drawn together by sheer luck I would never deserve or understand.

"Fresh start," she echoed, just as I slid into her body.

I knew the first time would be fast between us. I was already halfway there when I wasn't even touching her.

"Next time…" I let out a groan. "Because you feel so damn good I don't want to stop."

She dug her hands into my hair and pulled me down for a kiss as our bodies moved in sync, not once fighting but joining like it was the only thing they knew how to do really well.

I had seconds left.

I wanted to stretch them, I wanted to live in those seconds and concentrate on every single nerve ending was exploding with pleasure.

I angled myself deeper, she nearly leaped off the bed beneath me, and I found the spot I wanted.

"Oh, God." A muffled cry escaped her as she thrashed in pleasure under me. I felt her release shudder through her body and followed, unable to keep myself away from it any longer, away from her. She felt too good, it felt too right.

Panting, I flipped over onto my back and took her with me, still inside her, still feeling the aftershocks of our lovemaking.

It was on the tip of my tongue, but I wasn't the guy to confess love.

I was that guy with Jo, and look how that turned out.

Now I was cautious. And yet the words lingered on the tip of my tongue, to tell her that time didn't matter. I'd known my ex for a long time before we got married and look how that had turned out.

I knew Penny barely two weeks and already it felt different.

Because it was.

"Trevor?" She lay against my chest.

"Hmm?"

"I really like you."

"I really like you too." I played with her hair and then kissed her bare shoulder. "A lot."

"Daaaaaaddy!" Malcom wailed.

I've never had a woman jump off of me so fast.

She gave me a look of horror.

I grinned and just shook my head.

Red faced, she tiptoed into the bathroom while I quickly wrapped a towel around my waist. "Coming." I shrugged. "Duty calls."

Chapter Nineteen

Penelope

"How are you not sleeping?" I cuddled next to Trevor while he scribbled down a few more lyrics. He looked dead sexy in black-rimmed glasses, completely naked, with the sheets falling dangerously low on his hips as he continued writing.

"I'd be an idiot to sleep while you're in my bed, plus I slept most of the day because of how crappy I was feeling, and now inspiration." He grinned down at me. "You sleep, and I'll wake you up when I'm done."

"What are you writing?" I leaned up on my elbow and covered up my yawn with my hand.

"You," was all he said.

Stunned, I stared at him, waiting for him to elaborate, and when he didn't, I cleared my throat.

He grinned down at the notepad. "You inspired me."

"As in my boobs inspired you or something else?"

He burst out laughing. "While I do find your boobs especially inspirational…" He leaned down and kissed the side of my mouth. "I'm afraid I'm a bit more obsessed with this." He pressed his palm to the center of my chest. "And when I get obsessed, I write."

Tears filled my eyes. "You're—you're writing about me?"

"You. Your heart. Your beautiful soul. Yes."

"Are you done?" I moved slowly.

He scribbled something else down and studied the paper. "Why?"

"Because I'm about ready to seduce you for saying those words, for writing a song—you do realize how sexy that is, right?"

He shifted his gaze to me. "Yeah, I'm actually just writing my name over and over again. Took you long enough."

I tossed a pillow at him.

He caught it and then caught me by the wrists and pinned me against the mattress. "I'm kidding, I really am writing about you. People like songs that have passion, and I'm feeling very passionate—about you."

"Keep saying things like that and you won't get rid of me." I used a teasing tone, but part of me didn't want to tease.

He drew out a long kiss against my lips and whispered into the night, "Good."

I fell asleep against him, the heat of his body almost as addicting as his kiss.

I woke up with him wrapped around me.

With a smile on my face.

And contentment in my heart.

Being with him had been different, a good different. It felt like we fit and for the first time in years it was like the universe was putting me back on the right path, with him. Maybe I left Cunningham Falls for him, for this.

I knew I had to get up early to work, but I really, really wanted to stay in bed with him with the fireplace on.

Grumbling, I got out of his massive bed and started putting my clothes back on from the night before. At least the walk of shame was only a few doors down.

I smiled to myself and quickly ran to my room to get ready.

An hour later, the house was still dark. I tiptoed back to the master and found him sitting up writing again.

"Same song?"

"Yeah." He looked up and smiled. "You headed to work?"

"Somebody has to make coffee in the shit hole." I crossed my arms and gave him a little taunting look.

He groaned. "I'm sorry, it just came out. I think I was exhausted and—sorry, there's no excuse. It's a really small coffee shop—that happens to have the best coffee in Seaside. Forgive me?"

"You may need to earn more forgiveness." I raised my eyebrows then shot him a suggestive smile. "Hard labor. I'm owed more nakedness, don't you think?"

"As much as you want." He set his papers aside, stood, and slowly sauntered toward me. I knew he didn't do it on purpose. He oozed sexuality, and now that we'd been together, it was impacting me so severely that my thighs were trembling and my body was already buzzing with awareness of what it felt like to have him inside me, to hold him tight and cling to him like he was my universe. "You know…" He tilted my chin toward him. "I'm this close to asking how much they pay you so I can double it and keep you in bed."

"Ah, but the world needs me." I laughed. "Oh, and that's prostitution, Trevor, so maybe let's not get arrested today, okay?"

He laughed. "Fine. I'll see you at one?"

"Want me to grab Subway for the kids or something?"

"Sure, they'd love that." He reached for his wallet on the nightstand.

"Got my own money. I mean not millions like you but I can handle Subway." I chuckled and pointed at his notebook on the bed. "Your payment is getting that song done so I can hear it."

"Deal." He pressed a kiss to my mouth and then deepened it. God, his tongue was like velvet, how was that even possible?

I moaned into his mouth.

We broke apart, both of us out of breath.

"Going," I rasped. "Before I put my mouth—"

He kissed me again, interlocking his fingers with mine, pressing me against the bedpost. "How much time do we have?"

"Trev—" Oh, holy wow, okay, he had his hands in my leggings, already rolling them down my hips. "Maybe eight minutes."

"Mmm…" He flipped me around so I faced the bed post and thrust into me with one smooth movement that had me gasping for air. "The only way to start the morning."

"Except Folgers," I joked, and then nearly collapsed against him as I felt my release, quick and forceful.

"We should start every morning like this," he whispered against the crook of my neck.

"Deal." I drew a few deep breaths until I felt steadier.

And was still catching my breath by the time I made it to the coffee shop. Dani stopped by to grab coffees for the guys since they were headed into the studio later.

Just when I was about to leave my shift, a really pretty woman walked in.

She had jet black hair, perfectly pouted lips, and a tan that I knew had to be real, it was so golden.

"Wow." She scrunched up her nose and looked around the place. The woman looked like a Brazilian supermodel with nothing but good genes running through her body. "How cute."

"Um…thanks?" I smiled even though something felt off about her. "Is there something I can get for you?"

"Oh, sorry." She looked anything but. "I'm looking for a Penelope or Penny?"

I frowned. "That's me."

She stared, and stared harder. "You're kidding."

"Afraid not, what can I do for you?"

Her smile grew to epic proportions. "Oh, honey."

"Oh, honey? What?"

"You know—" She clasped her hands in front of her then turned on her heel. "Never mind, problem solved. Have a good day, Penelope. I know I will!"

"'Kay." I shook my head. Stupid actresses and models swarming the area to get a look at A list actors. I rolled my eyes and made myself a coffee, then ran to Subway to grab some sandwiches. I was about ten minutes late by the time I got to Trevor's.

A car I didn't recognize was parked in front. Maybe one of the guys whose expensive car I hadn't seen yet.

This one was a nice red Maserati SUV.

I'd stopped knocking on the door by day three, but when I went to open it, it was locked.

Forced to knock, I set my things on the ground in front of me and did just that.

The door swung open.

Rude woman from the coffee shop stood there in her leather dress and black painted fingernails that matched her hair, bright red lipstick, perfect tan, and little booties hugging her what I imagined would be perfect feet. "Ah, the nanny's here."

"That's me," I said through clenched teeth. "I'm sorry, but what are you doing here? Oh no! The kids!" I shoved past her, worry about the strange woman gone as I saw each of the kids sitting at the table eating pizza.

"Penny!" they said in unison.

"Hey, guys!" They were fine. In fact, they looked more than fine. "Where's your dad?"

"Oh, he went to the studio." The woman crossed her arms. "You get the day off, yay."

"I'm sorry, but I'm not leaving you with the kids alone. I don't know you." I crossed my arms to mirror her. "Unless I hear it from Trevor—"

"Mommy!" Bella giggled. "Can you get me some more Sprite?"

"Sure, honey." She winked and went over to the fridge to grab some Sprite, Sprite that I'd purchased for the kids for when they were allowed to have soda.

It was next to the gallon of milk I'd gotten because Trevor had forgotten.

A golf ball lodged in my throat as I watched this strange woman, Trevor's ex-wife, move through the house like she'd been the one to make it a home. When I knew that in the last two weeks I'd done more than she ever had.

"What are you doing here?" I asked boldly.

"Being a parent," she fired back. "And a wife."

My jaw went slack. "Can I talk to you for a minute?"

"Sure." She gave Bella her pop. "Eric, help your sister open it. No spills."

"Okay." He was the only one who seemed mildly upset over the pizza. And suddenly the Subway I'd bought them felt pathetic and stupid.

So did my cheap leggings and my long-sleeve Henley.

And the stupid beanie I'd put on.

The lip gloss I'd purchased at Sephora.

Everything felt…less than.

And I hated it.

Trevor had never made me feel that way.

This woman did with not so much as a word.

"You can't just say things like that," I whispered in a low voice. "The kids, they miss you—"

"I'm going to stop you right there, Penny." She held up her hand like I was a petulant child. "Those kids are mine, not yours. This life is mine, not yours. Got it? I'm their mother, not you. And Trevor and I are still working through some things."

That was when I saw the ring.

On her left hand.

It was so many karats that I was sure it cramped the muscles on that side of her body because of the weight.

It was beautiful.

It was just like her.

I shook my head, tears filling my eyes.

"Sweetie, we're talking about Trevor Wood here. Did you really think that he was going to go for—" She narrowed her eyes in disbelief as her gaze raked over me. "Whatever you have going on?"

I felt that stare all the way into my Nikes.

"That's not—" I prayed for patience. "That's not what I mean. Trevor said you guys are divorced, ergo, you can't come in here randomly and give the children hope."

There, that sounded good.

"Oh, sweetie, he didn't tell you, did he? Shame." Her grin was pure evil. "I haven't signed shit. We're legally separated. Not. Divorced."

The room started spinning.

The kids laughed in the distance.

And she stared at me like she'd won, when I wasn't even aware I was in a game. Let alone racing her.

"I'll just..." I moved past her. "Kids? If you need anything, you have my number, okay?"

"Okay!" they chirped.

I shared a look with Eric, but he quickly averted his eyes.

Bella grinned at me. "Isn't it great, Penny? Mommy's back!"

"It's...something." I forced a smile that felt more like my face was on the verge of breaking into a million pieces and excused myself from the house.

I grabbed the Subway food and put it back in my car.

With shaking hands, I took a sip of coffee, only to have it spill down the front of my shirt.

And then I burst into tears and called the only person who could give me answers.

Only to have it go straight to voicemail.

Chapter Twenty

Trevor

"Sorry I'm late." I breezed into the room and put my phone on silent, grabbed a pair of headphones and sat down. "Penny wasn't back yet, and then my worst nightmare showed up out of the blue on my doorstep..." I groaned into my hands. "She's like the devil but worse."

Drew shrugged and strummed his guitar. "You're the douche that didn't listen to us when we said she tried to get Ty to sleep with her at least a dozen times before you put a ring on it."

"Don't remind me." I tossed a drumstick in the air.

"So did she stay?"

I let out a rough exhale. "Unfortunately. I'm hoping if I play nice, she'll give me full custody. The divorce just went through last month, man, but she's missed every court date and the law says she has to be present. She has one more chance, then the kids are mine. I'm hoping they scare her away."

Drew stared me down like I'd grown three heads. "I'm sorry. Am I to assume that she's at the house right now?"

"What the hell was I supposed to do? Kick her out? Bella burst into tears and ran into her arms. She brought pizza, see? The devil incarnate! Malcom looked ready to worship her, and Eric smiled for the first time all day!"

Ty walked into the room. "Sorry, I was eavesdropping—know what? Actually I'm not sorry. Are you insane?"

"What?" Heat crept up the back of my neck, that and a shit ton of anxiety. "Could you guys just explain?"

Will came over the studio com. "Guilty of eavesdropping too. Dude, you need to go back to the house now."

"Guys, she's their mom. They're not going to set her on fire even if she deserves it."

"Right…" Will said through the mic and then shook his head and walked into the main part of the studio and pulled out a chair. "Look, Drew and I have experience with this sort of manipulation." Drew just snorted and gave a nod. Good to know they were at least speaking without cussing each other out or pulling out dicks and measuring. "Hollywood bitches be bitches."

"You sound so white," Ty muttered.

"Accurate, however," Drew pointed out. "And as much as it pains me to give Will any credit where he looks better in public—he's a hundred percent right. Okay, so even if you aren't concerned that your ex might take off with the kids, what do you think's gonna happen the minute Penelope shows up to do her job?"

"She'll do her job." I said dumbly. "I mean I don't exactly trust Jo to stay put, she's the type of parent that would take off, remember? Bored with this life? She was a good mom until she just quit being a mom, it didn't help that she started using drugs with whatever that dick's name is."

"My point exactly." Will sighed like he was stressed out when I was sweating bullets. "Penelope isn't used to that sort of thing. To guys like us, we just laugh it off and go 'wow, glad I'm not married to that.' She won't know what's real and what's not real." He shot me a pointed stare. "Then again, if you haven't slept with her, I guess that's not a problem—"

I shot to my feet and reached for the front of his T-shirt.

Will's eyebrows shot up. "I thought you were the least violent of the bunch."

"Holy shit." Drew sounded like he was seconds from shitting his pants. "You slept with her, you dirty dog, up top!"

I ignored his hand.

Shoved Will away.

And reached for my phone.

I had two missed calls from Penelope.

And five from my own kids.

I quickly dialed the emergency phone I'd given Eric and waited.

When he answered, I heard crying in the background and then screaming. "Wake up, wake up!"

"Eric, buddy, what's going on?" I felt myself pale as all of the guys stood, like they were ready to go to war for me.

"Mom, she's sick, I don't know. She told us to eat our pizza and made Penny sad, and I knew it was a trick because then she went into the bathroom and didn't come out for a really long time."

"Is she still there?" I was already headed out of the studio, with all of my bandmates on my heels.

"Yeah, but she's super sleepy and her eyes look funny, and she yelled at Bella for ruining her buzz. Is that bad?"

Son of a bitch!

I jumped in my SUV and noticed that all the guys got in their cars too.

"Stay on the phone with me, buddy, I'm headed there now."

"Wait, someone's at the door...."

"DON'T ANSWER THE DOOR!" I roared.

But it was too late.

I saw my life flash before my eyes in those few seconds.

I felt my heart shatter into a billion pieces.

Amazing how the one person you imagined you'll build your life with—is the very one who brings it crashing down around you.

I gripped the steering wheel and hit the accelerator, breaking every law in downtown Seaside, and prayed he didn't answer the damn door.

Chapter Twenty-One

Penelope

I made it maybe seven minutes past their house when I stopped in the middle of the road and just stared at the four-way stop.

I had nowhere to go.

My shift was done.

All my stuff was currently in a house that I couldn't live in.

And the rest of my things were at Trevor's.

I could have gone shopping, I guess.

Headed to Dani's.

I could have done a lot of things.

But part of me felt like I was running away from a fight.

Part of me felt like I was doing to those kids exactly what their mother had done to them.

I was leaving my job.

Leaving my job.

But Trevor hadn't asked me to.

No, his bitch of an ex or whatever she was did.

What if something happened to the kids?

She hadn't been parenting them for the last year. Did she know about Bella's allergies? Or about Eric's night terrors? Malcom's fear of toothbrushes?

The more I thought about it, the sicker I felt, until I turned the car around, ignoring all the signs in my heart that told me I was being used and being stupid.

Because if I'd learned nothing else in the last few weeks, it was that the kids trumped all.

And I would never forgive myself if anything happened.

I pulled to the front of the house, took a few deep breaths and walked up the walkway, knocked twice, then let myself in.

Why hadn't she locked the door?

That was what you did when you had kids!

The minute I opened the door, Eric dropped the phone in his hand and burst into tears, wrapping his little arms around me. "I'm so scared."

"It's going to be okay, buddy." Terror seized my very soul as I looked around the room. The horrible woman was sprawled on the floor, her head laying on the coffee table, an empty smile on her gaping mouth. I could barely see her eyes. She squinted at me like she was looking at the sun. "What happened?"

Soon I had Bella attached to the other side of me, Malcom squeezing in next to Eric, and the woman who shall not be named laughing hysterically from the floor. Her head fell back to the table. "God, they get loud when they get older, right? Thought pizza would at least keep them occupied for a few hours."

"Kids eat fast," I said, ready to slap her across the face and call the police. "What's wrong with you?"

Her head lolled to the side and then she pointed at me, her hand dropping to her side limply, as if she didn't have the energy to lift it anymore. "You're nothing like the women those guys date."

My eyebrows shot up. "From where I stand, that's a pretty nice compliment, thank you."

"Bitch." She tried to stand.

A soft wind could blow her over.

I knew she couldn't hurt us, but I also knew the scars that could run deep in a kid's mind when they saw their mom not acting normal.

So I lied.

Not for her.

For them.

"Your mom is probably catching what your dad had." I forced a smile. "Why don't we go upstairs and watch a movie while she sleeps it off?"

She gave another delirious laugh from her spot on the floor.

Eric put his hand in mine, while I picked up Bella, holding her on one hip. Malcom grabbed Eric's hand, and all of us walked upstairs to shut out the rest of the world.

I locked the door.

And immediately called Drew, knowing that he would at least be with Trevor and be able to let him know.

He answered on the first ring. "Kinda busy, Penny!"

"I'm at the house," I blurted. "Trevor's—his wife is downstairs, high out of her mind," I whispered into the phone. "I took the kids upstairs and the room's locked and—" Footsteps pounded outside the door. "—someone's coming."

"Open the door, Penny." Trevor's voice sounded from the other side.

I scrambled over and unlocked the door.

Trevor bypassed me, making a beeline for his kids. "Are you okay?" He cupped Eric's face and started examining it like he'd been in a fight. "Eric?"

Eric's eyes filled with tears. "I was so scared, and I heard Penny. She came back, Dad." He fell apart in his dad's arms. "Dad, Penny came back for us."

"Yes." Trevor rocked Eric back and forth as Bella and Malcom surrounded them. "She did."

Chapter Twenty-Two

Trevor

I called the police.

I asked them to be discreet.

And I watched them handcuff my ex-wife for possession. Heroin, Oxy, and a few other gems that were stuffed in her purse.

Apparently, her latest flame left her for someone else, and the minute she heard that I was recording in Seaside and had been linked somehow to Penny, she'd taken the first flight out.

To fight for her family.

Or so she said and believed.

But fighting shouldn't include getting high in front of your kids or traumatizing them.

It didn't include buying their love with pizza and gifts, empty promises and smiles.

I was sick.

So sick.

Her lies were like a poison. She dug her talons into everything perfect in my life and spread like a darkness I couldn't stop.

I hated her.

So. Much.

The guys stayed over while I talked with the police. Penny didn't leave the kids' sides and I noticed a few times how Bella would tug on Penny's arm and she would just naturally lift her off her feet and hold her or play with her hair while she walked around the kitchen.

If Jo was my nightmare.

Penny was my dream.

I just didn't know how to navigate it, especially considering I had nothing to offer but a struggling, traumatized family, myself included.

When the police finally left and the house was once again silent, when the kids were put to bed with strict instructions to never ever answer the door unless an adult was home…

I exhaled.

And then I didn't think. With purposeful steps, I walked toward Penny. She was cleaning up all the leftover pizza, putting things back in the cupboards, and now she was elbow deep in the sink, surrounded by dirty dishes since the dishwasher was probably still full.

I'd never seen anyone so stunning in my entire life.

I wrapped my arms around her and felt time stop as her body stiffened.

"I'm only going to say this once." My heart thudded wildly against my chest. "I would be lost without you. We would be lost without you. Stay."

I could feel her body sway, knew that she was fighting something, most likely doubt—about us, about what any of this chaos meant.

"Stay," I said again and then slowly turned her to face me.

Water ran down her hands, tears filled her eyes.

"For the record, I'm not married. She signed the divorce papers and the only reason I left her with the kids today was because I knew you would be on your way and I underestimated the hate in her heart. She told me she was in town for a day before leaving and begged to have some time with the kids. I told her you were bringing lunch so to check with you first…" I tilted my head. "I gave her your number and everything and then totally spaced the rest when Drew texted and said he had a breakthrough on one of our tracks. Plus, I know it's stupid, but she had one final thing to dangle in front of me, and that's one hundred percent custody, so I let her, and I shouldn't have." My voice cracked. "Because I can't imagine what could have happened, what would have happened had you not come back."

"But I did." Her voice was hoarse, full of pain. "I came back. For them."

"I'll never be able to repay you. I can't say I'm sorry enough. I should have called you, should have warned you, I just—you have to believe me, what you saw today, that's not always been her. She was present. She wasn't the best but she wasn't ever cruel to others, she wouldn't endanger her kids. Ignore them? Yes. Endanger them? No."

"Drugs…" Penny sighed. "They let you justify everything and take responsibility for nothing."

"Thank you." I kissed the tip of her nose, then her forehead. "Thank you…for being here, for being part of us."

"Am I?" She looked up at me, her eyes questioning. "I mean, what are we doing here? The twins start school in a couple of weeks, Bella starts pre-school sooner than that, and I'm just—"

I silenced her with a kiss. And then another when she tried to protest.

And then I lifted her onto the counter and pulled her against me, wrapping her legs around me. "You were saying?"

"I'm…" Her dazed expression darkened. "You can't just kiss it away, Trevor. I'm furious with you!"

I grinned "Because you thought I was still married and sleeping with you?"

Her cheeks pinked. "Well, that and you should have called. That was stupid, so stupid. Ugh, I hate men." She let out a little grumble. "Women are evil, horrible creatures."

My eyebrows shot up.

"I mean not all women, but she's one of those people, and the poor kids." Tears filled her eyes again. "I was so angry with her, so angry, I wanted to kill her, Trevor. I'm not a violent person, but I would have ended her life for making them afraid, for letting them down."

I swiped the tears from her cheeks. "And that's exactly what makes you such an incredible person, what will make you an amazing mom…"

I kissed her again.

She wrapped her arms around my neck and pulled back, our foreheads touching. "I don't know how to navigate this. It's not like they have a rule book for dating rock stars."

"Did you just feed my ego a rock star compliment?"

"Shut up."

I pulled her in for another kiss, smiling against her pout. "We take it a day at a time. When they start school, they start school. Think of it this way. They're going to have after-school activities, practices, plays, macaroni necklaces—and you'll be there for it all."

"What makes you so sure?" she whispered.

"Because you stayed when any normal person would have run away, pissed at the world. Because you fought for them before you fought for you. And because when I look up at the stars, you remind me that no matter how secure they may look—they still fall. And sometimes in falling, you find your forever."

"Are you saying you fell?" She bit down on her bottom lip, a hopeful look in her eyes.

"I fell the first day I saw you. I'm still falling. I don't ever want to stop. I pray there's never a day I wake up and realize I'm on the ground—because I want to be in a constant state of falling in love with you."

She sucked in a sharp breath, I kissed her again.

I wiped her tears and carried her up the stairs.

Past my children's rooms.

As visions of a life with her danced in my head.

As songs I hadn't yet written played in perfect cadence.

As the warmth of her body gave me hope.

As I carried her into a bedroom I hoped one day to call ours.

And kissed her deep, hard.

She didn't protest when I pulled the clothes from her body, leaving nothing behind, as I took in her smooth skin and then pulled her onto the bed and covered my body with hers. "This time, I go slow."

"Think you'll last?" she teased.

"That's it." I reached for a pillow but she'd already flipped me onto my back. I let her, obviously, and grinned up at her. "What are you going to do?"

"Kiss you." She leaned down, touching our lips together. "Everywhere I want."

"No complaints here." I watched her devour me with her eyes, and then felt her do the same with her mouth. She gripped me, and I slapped her hand away because I wanted more than that. "Together, I want us together, I want to watch us together."

I pulled her onto me, my hands on her hips. She slid over me and let out a large gasp while she moved in perfect rhythm.

A rhythm I didn't realize had been in my heart for years.

A rhythm that promised forever.

That felt so right I couldn't breathe.

"Tell me I get to keep you." We locked eyes.

She quickened her pace, I caught her hips rocking her faster, needing to feel the realness between us. "On one condition...."

"What's that?"

"You make Drew sign a poster."

"You'll pay for that." I couldn't even pretend to be mad, she felt too damn good. "But later, much later. Right now, I just want you, and us."

"Us," she agreed.

And I followed her over the cliff with a smile on my face.

Chapter Twenty-Three

Penelope

6 Months Later

"He's too sexy, his sweat is sexy, I both hate and love this," I murmured as I stood backstage watching all the girls scream Trevor's name as he walked around shirtless with low slung jeans and paint all over his six pack.

Was that paint edible?

Would it be weird to ask if he could bring it home?

Will's wife Angelica elbowed me and then burst out laughing. "It's hard some days. Just remember who gets him at night."

"Preach." Alyssa, Demetri's wife, currently pregnant with triplets, did an awkward little jig and then elbowed Nat, who was currently salivating over her own husband, Alec.

Jaymeson held up his phone. "Smile, ladies."

We all grinned.

He took the picture, then dropped his hand. "The concert's going over."

"They sold out all six shows," I pointed out. "They just want to give them their money's worth."

Zane, or Saint as he was known, ran out to the middle of the stage and fell to his knees as Alec and Demetri took the mic, and then the rest of Adrenaline joined in.

Zane, Adrenaline, and AD2. They'd added more tour stops after last year's Grammys.

And now I knew why.

I'd seen their shows on TV.

Never in person.

It was almost addicting the way they all performed, but I had eyes for my man and my man only.

The song ended, and Trevor threw his sticks into the crowd. They all went wild, and the guys ran off stage.

I was pulled into the biggest, messiest hug ever and that was saying a lot since I was living with three children and a guy who constantly had some sort of food substance on his person.

"Hey"—Trevor grinned down at me—"I have a surprise for you."

"Really?"

"Yup."

I looked behind him. Malcom, Eric, and Bella were all on stage. The twins had tuxes on, and Bella was in a gorgeous white dress.

"What's going on?"

"Something very important." Trevor put on a shirt and pulled me onto the stage, the crowd erupting with screams and shrieks.

I almost puked.

He grabbed a microphone. "Bella, Eric, Malcom, will you help Dad?"

He held out the microphone to Eric. "Will."

Malcom followed and giggled. "You."

"Marry," Bella screamed.

And then Trevor dropped to one knee and rasped, "Us?"

I lost it.

And I hugged the kids first.

Much to the amusement of probably everyone in the stadium.

And then Trevor laughed in the microphone. "You'd think she's more excited about the package deal than the actual deal!"

Everyone joined in laughing.

And then I grabbed the microphone and said, "Yes. I say yes to us."

"So you're staying?"

"Forever," I said through sloppy tears as tiny arms wrapped around my waist and held on tight.

That was when I noticed that there was no black shirt hanging off

Bella or even being held by someone off stage.

No, tonight, she had her security.

Us.

Music started, and Trevor grabbed a microphone.

The crowd held up their cell phones while AD2 returned to the stage with the rest of Adrenaline.

"Let me tell you a story, one that's hard to tell. You think we've got it made, you don't see how the lights fade, and then there's nothing, no story, no forever, until you realize that what you thought was true was false, what's false is true." He beamed at me, while the kids held my hands, and we swayed to the music moving to the side of the stage. It was a new song, one I hadn't heard before Trevor was singing, not just singing, nailing it. "Let me tell you a story, one that's hard to tell. I met the perfect girl, and then I really fell. But I hit the ground running, didn't look behind, didn't realize forever was never on her mind. The truth is sometimes hard to see, but it has never been so clear, until I met a dream. She told me we were worth it, despite the baggage made, and when I kissed her soft lips, I knew I'd been changed inside. Because all...stars...fall." The chorus slowed. Tears ran down my cheeks. "All. Stars. Fall. The biggest truth of my life, one that's hard and true, is that all the stars fell and led me back to you."

The crowd went wild.

I couldn't see the stage.

But I felt his words.

And the small hands around me.

I felt his love.

And my fresh start.

In an Us.

* * * *

Also from 1001 Dark Nights and Rachel Van Dyken, discover Abandon and Envy.

Sign up for the 1001 Dark Nights Newsletter
and be entered to win a Tiffany Lock necklace.

There's a contest every quarter!

Go to www.1001DarkNights.com to subscribe.

As a bonus, all subscribers can download
FIVE FREE exclusive books!

Discover the Kristen Proby Crossover Collection

Soaring with Fallon: A Big Sky Novel
By Kristen Proby

Fallon McCarthy has climbed the corporate ladder. She's had the office with the view, the staff, and the plaque on her door. The unexpected loss of her grandmother taught her that there's more to life than meetings and conference calls, so she quit, and is happy to be a nomad, checking off items on her bucket list as she takes jobs teaching yoga in each place she lands in. She's happy being free, and has no interest in being tied down.

When Noah King gets the call that an eagle has been injured, he's not expecting to find a beautiful stranger standing vigil when he arrives. Rehabilitating birds of prey is Noah's passion, it's what he lives for, and he doesn't have time for a nosy woman who's suddenly taken an interest in Spread Your Wings sanctuary.

But Fallon's gentle nature, and the way she makes him laugh, and *feel* again draws him in. When it comes time for Fallon to move on, will Noah's love be enough for her to stay, or will he have to find the strength to let her fly?

* * * *

Wicked Force: A Wicked Horse Vegas/Big Sky Novella
By Sawyer Bennett

From *New York Times* and *USA Today* bestselling author Sawyer Bennett...

Joslyn Meyers has taken the celebrity world by storm, drawing the attention of millions. But one fan's affections has gone too far, and she's running to the one place she hopes he'll never find her – back home to Cunningham Falls.

Kynan McGrath leads The Jameson Group, a world-class security organization, and he's ready to do what it takes to keep Joslyn safe, even if it means giving up his own life in return. The one thing he's not prepared to lose, though, is his heart.

* * * *

Crazy Imperfect Love: A Dirty Dicks/Big Sky Novella
By KL Grayson

From *USA Today* bestselling author KL Grayson...

Abigail Darwin needs one thing in life: consistency. Okay, make that two things: consistency and order. Tired of being shackled to her obsessive-compulsive mind, Abigail is determined to break free. Which is why she's shaking things up.

Fresh out of nursing school, she takes a traveling nurse position. A new job in a new city every few months? That's a sure-fire way to keep her from settling down and falling into old habits. First stop, Cunningham Falls, Montana.

The only problem? She didn't plan on falling in love with the quaint little town, and she sure as heck didn't plan on falling for its resident surgeon, Dr. Drake Merritt.

Laid back, messy, and spontaneous, Drake is everything she's not. But he is completely smitten by the new, quirky nurse working on the med-surg floor of the hospital.

Abby puts up a good fight, but Drake is determined to break through her carefully erected walls to find out what makes her tick. And sigh and moan and smile and laugh. Because he really loves her laugh.

But falling in love isn't part of Abby's plan. Will Drake have what it takes to convince her that the best things in life come from doing what scares us the most?

* * * *

Worth Fighting For: A Warrior Fight Club/Big Sky Novella
By Laura Kaye

From *New York Times* and *USA Today* bestselling author Laura Kaye...

Getting in deep has never felt this good...

Commercial diving instructor Tara Hunter nearly lost everything in an accident that saw her medically discharged from the navy. With the help of the Warrior Fight Club, she's fought hard to overcome her fears and get back in the water where she's always felt most at home. At work, she's tough, serious, and doesn't tolerate distractions. Which is why finding her gorgeous one-night stand on her new dive team is such a problem.

Former navy deep-sea diver Jesse Anderson just can't seem to stop making mistakes—the latest being the hot-as-hell night he'd spent with his new partner. This job is his second chance, and Jesse knows he shouldn't mix business with pleasure. But spending every day with Tara's smart mouth and sexy curves makes her so damn hard to resist.

Joining a wounded warrior MMA training program seems like the perfect way to blow off steam—until Jesse finds that Tara belongs too. Now they're getting in deep and taking each other down day and night, and even though it breaks all the rules, their inescapable attraction might just be the only thing truly worth fighting for.

* * * *

Nothing Without You: A Forever Yours/Big Sky Novella
By Monica Murphy

From *New York Times* and *USA Today* bestselling author Monica Murphy...

Designing wedding cakes is Maisey Henderson's passion. She puts her heart and soul into every cake she makes, especially since she's such a believer in true love. But then Tucker McCloud rolls back into town, reminding her that love is a complete joke. The pro football player is the hottest thing to come out of Cunningham Falls—and the boy who broke Maisey's heart back in high school.

He claims he wants another chance. She says absolutely not. But Maisey's refusal is the ultimate challenge to Tucker. Life is a game, and Tucker's playing to win Maisey's heart—forever.

* * * *

All Stars Fall: A Seaside Pictures/Big Sky Novella
By Rachel Van Dyken

From *New York Times* and *USA Today* bestselling author Rachel Van Dyken…

She *left*.
Two words I can't really get out of my head.
She left *us*.
Three more words that make it that much worse.
Three being another word I can't seem to wrap my mind around.
Three kids under the age of six, and she left because she missed it. Because her dream had never been to have a family, no her dream had been to marry a rockstar and live the high life.

Moving my recording studio to Seaside Oregon seems like the best idea in the world right now especially since Seaside Oregon has turned into the place for celebrities to stay and raise families in between touring and producing. It would be lucrative to make the move, but I'm doing it for my kids because they need normal, they deserve normal. And me? Well, I just need a break and help, that too. I need a sitter and fast. Someone who won't flip me off when I ask them to sign an Iron Clad NDA, someone who won't sell our pictures to the press, and most of all? Someone who looks absolutely nothing like my ex-wife.

He's tall.
That was my first instinct when I saw the notorious Trevor Wood, drummer for the rock band Adrenaline, in the local coffee shop. He ordered a tall black coffee which made me smirk, and five minutes later I somehow agreed to interview for a nanny position. I couldn't help it; the smaller one had gum stuck in her hair while the eldest was standing on his feet and asking where babies came from. He looked so pathetic, so damn sexy and pathetic that rather than be star-struck, I took pity. I knew though; I knew the minute I signed that NDA, the minute our fingers brushed and my body became insanely aware of how close he was—I was in dangerous territory, I just didn't know how dangerous

until it was too late. Until I fell for the star and realized that no matter how high they are in the sky—they're still human and fall just as hard.

* * * *

Hold On: A Play On/Big Sky Novella
By Samantha Young

From *New York Times* and *USA Today* bestselling author Samantha Young…

Autumn O'Dea has always tried to see the best in people while her big brother, Killian, has always tried to protect her from the worst. While their lonely upbringing made Killian a cynic, it isn't in Autumn's nature to be anything but warm and open. However, after a series of relationship disasters and the unsettling realization that she's drifting aimlessly through life, Autumn wonders if she's left herself too vulnerable to the world. Deciding some distance from the security blanket of her brother and an unmotivated life in Glasgow is exactly what she needs to find herself, Autumn takes up her friend's offer to stay at a ski resort in the snowy hills of Montana. Some guy-free alone time on Whitetail Mountain sounds just the thing to get to know herself better.

However, she wasn't counting on colliding into sexy Grayson King on the slopes. Autumn has never met anyone like Gray. Confident, smart, with a wicked sense of humor, he makes the men she dated seem like boys. Her attraction to him immediately puts her on the defense because being open-hearted in the past has only gotten it broken. Yet it becomes increasingly difficult to resist a man who is not only determined to seduce her, but adamant about helping her find her purpose in life and embrace the person she is. Autumn knows she shouldn't fall for Gray. It can only end badly. After all their lives are divided by an ocean and their inevitable separation is just another heart break away…

Discover 1001 Dark Nights Collection Six

DRAGON CLAIMED by Donna Grant
A Dark Kings Novella

ASHES TO INK by Carrie Ann Ryan
A Montgomery Ink: Colorado Springs Novella

ENSNARED by Elisabeth Naughton
An Eternal Guardians Novella

EVERMORE by Corinne Michaels
A Salvation Series Novella

VENGEANCE by Rebecca Zanetti
A Dark Protectors/Rebels Novella

ELI'S TRIUMPH by Joanna Wylde
A Reapers MC Novella

CIPHER by Larissa Ione
A Demonica Underworld Novella

RESCUING MACIE by Susan Stoker
A Delta Force Heroes Novella

ENCHANTED by Lexi Blake
A Masters and Mercenaries Novella

TAKE THE BRIDE by Carly Phillips
A Knight Brothers Novella

INDULGE ME by J. Kenner
A Stark Ever After Novella

THE KING by Jennifer L. Armentrout
A Wicked Novella

QUIET MAN by Kristen Ashley
A Dream Man Novella

ABANDON by Rachel Van Dyken
A Seaside Pictures Novella

THE OPEN DOOR by Laurelin Paige
A Found Duet Novella

CLOSER by Kylie Scott
A Stage Dive Novella

SOMETHING JUST LIKE THIS by Jennifer Probst
A Stay Novella

BLOOD NIGHT by Heather Graham
A Krewe of Hunters Novella

TWIST OF FATE by Jill Shalvis
A Heartbreaker Bay Novella

MORE THAN PLEASURE YOU by Shayla Black
A More Than Words Novella

WONDER WITH ME by Kristen Proby
A With Me In Seattle Novella

THE DARKEST ASSASSIN by Gena Showalter
A Lords of the Underworld Novella

Also from 1001 Dark Nights:
DAMIEN by J. Kenner
A Stark Novel

About Rachel Van Dyken

Rachel Van Dyken is the *New York Times, Wall Street Journal,* and *USA TODAY* Bestselling author of regency and contemporary romances. When she's not writing you can find her drinking coffee at Starbucks and plotting her next book while watching The Bachelor.

She keeps her home in Idaho with her Husband and, adorable son. She loves to hear from readers!

For more information, visit her website at
http://rachelvandykenauthor.com

Discover More Rachel Van Dyken

Abandon
A Seaside Pictures Novella
By Rachel Van Dyken
Coming August 27, 2019

From *New York Times* and *USA Today* bestselling author Rachel Van Dyken comes a new story in her Seaside Pictures series…

It's not every day you're slapped on stage by two different women you've been dating for the last year.

I know what you're thinking. What sort of ballsy woman gets on stage and slaps a rockstar? Does nobody have self-control anymore? It may have been the talk of the Grammy's.

Oh, yeah, forgot to mention that. I, Ty Cuban, was taken down by two psychotic women in front of the entire world. Lucky for us the audience thought it was part of the breakup song my band and I had just finished performing. I was thirty-three, hardly ready to settle down.

Except now it's getting forced on me. Seaside, Oregon. My band mates were more than happy to settle down, dig their roots into the sand, and start popping out kids. Meanwhile I was still enjoying life.

Until now. Until my forced hiatus teaching freaking guitar lessons at the local studio for the next two months. Part of my punishment, do something for the community while I think deep thoughts about all my life choices.

Sixty days of hell.

It doesn't help that the other volunteer is a past flame that literally looks at me as if I've sold my soul to the devil. She has the voice of an angel and looks to kill—I would know, because she looks ready to kill me every second of every day. I broke her heart when we were on tour together a decade ago.

I'm ready to put the past behind us. She's ready to run me over with her car then stand on top of it and strum her guitar with glee.

Sixty days. I can do anything for sixty days. Including making the sexy Von Abigail fall for me all over again. This time for good.

Damn, maybe there's something in the water.

* * * *

Envy
An Eagle Elite Novella
By Rachel Van Dyken
Now Available

From *New York Times and USA Today* bestselling author Rachel Van Dyken comes a new story in her Eagle Elite series…

Every family has rules, the mafia just has more....
Do not speak to the bosses unless spoken to.
Do not make eye contact unless you want to die.
And above all else, do not fall in love.
Renee Cassani's future is set.
Her betrothal is set.
Her life, after nannying for the five families for the summer, is set.
Somebody should have told Vic Colezan that.
He's a man who doesn't take no for an answer.
And he only wants one thing.
Her.
Somebody should have told Renee that her bodyguard needed as much discipline as the kids she was nannying.
Good thing Vic has a firm hand.

Risky Play
Red Card Book 1
By Rachel Van Dyken
Coming March 19, 2019

Even one-night stands deserve a second chance in *New York Times* bestselling author Rachel Van Dyken's novel of sporting desire.

What else can a virgin do when she's ditched at the altar? Seattle heiress Mackenzie Dupont is treating herself to a single-girl honeymoon in Mexico and a desire to relinquish her innocence to a gorgeous one-night stand. Fake names. True pleasure. But when she wakes up alone, Mackenzie realizes just how much anger is left in her broken heart.

Suffering a tragic personal loss, pro soccer player Slade Rodriguez has his reasons for vanishing without a goodbye. Right or wrong, he's blaming the beautiful and infuriating stranger he never wants to see again. They're both in for a shock when Mackenzie shows up as his new personal assistant. And they both have a lot to learn about each other. Because they share more than they could possibly know, including a common enemy who's playing his own games. And he's not afraid to get dirty.

Now there's only one way Mackenzie and Slade can win: to trust in each other and to stop hiding from the lies they've told, the secrets they've kept, the mistakes they've made, and the attraction that still burns between them.

* * * *

"WAKE UP!" a voice screeched next to me.

I jerked to attention as the woman tugged down my headphones and reached for my hand. "Engine failure!"

"Stop yelling." I pressed a hand to my temple as I looked around the cabin. Everyone seemed to be panicked and staring at the flight attendant like she was going to somehow fix this or hand out parachutes.

"This is your captain," crackled a reasonably calm voice over the loudspeaker. "We've lost one engine, but luckily we're a few miles out from the Puerto Vallarta airport. Just hang tight and try to relax. We'll be making an emergency landing in the next ten minutes." Oxygen masks tumbled from the panel above us. The captain came back on. "Flight attendants, prepare the cabin, and buckle up."

The woman next to me was pale as a ghost. "This!" She held her head in her hands. "It can't end like this! I'm not ready, you hear me, universe!" She clenched her fists. "I was left at the altar, this is unfair! Completely unfair!"

"Uh, can I get you something?" I whispered to her in an effort to both calm her and try to get her to put the mask over her nose and mouth. "To help you calm down and stop talking to yourself?"

"One thing." Her light-blue eyes met mine as an electrical charge pulsed between our bodies.

The plane shook and dove a few hundred feet. I grabbed her hand and rubbed it with my thumb.

She shrieked and reached for my shirt, gripping it with both hands while her eyes frantically searched mine for confirmation everything was going to be okay.

The plane plummeted again.

I gripped her hands, needing the distraction just as much, as a loud noise filled the cabin.

"Answer this question: What one thing do you regret?" she said in a voice that sounded like failure, like giving up, like the world was against her in every single way.

"Just one?" I tried to make light of the conversation even though my adrenaline was spiking like I'd just started the championship match. The plane kept diving at rapid speeds, causing my stomach to lurch. We needed to get our masks on, but getting them on seemed like it would only make her more frantic, and I needed her calm. I wasn't sure why—I just did. Maybe because her touch was calming me. Maybe because it was the first time I'd touched another woman since being betrayed by the one I thought I loved.

"One." She nodded more calmly now.

I kept my eyes locked on hers. "I would have drunk all the wine. You were right, it deserved more than a 'good.'"

Her eyes lit up like I'd just told her she was the most beautiful woman I'd ever seen, which wasn't too far off the mark. From her caramel-colored hair to her almost too-big eyes to the wide smile on her pillow-like lips, I could imagine many things I'd rather be doing with her than talking.

"Really?"

"Really." I nodded. "Your turn."

The plane dipped, and she sent a worried glance toward the cockpit.

"Hey." I grabbed her chin. "It's going to be fine, pilots are trained for this. Just focus on me, on my voice. Can you do that?"

She swallowed, closed her eyes, then nodded. "Yes, I can do that."

"Good." I dropped my hand as an alarm sounded around the plane. The flight attendants ran to their spots as we lost more elevation. I could see the mountains in the window right along with civilization; we were at least ten thousand feet, maybe lower. The airport must be nearby.

"I would have said no," she finally answered.

"Said no?" I repeated, confused.

"To Alton, when he asked me if I loved him. I would have said no. I would have said not the way you deserve, and I would have walked away."

Heavy.

My eyes briefly scanned her left hand. No ring.

"And then"—she kept talking—"I think I would have kissed you."

My eyebrows shot up as a smile spread across my face despite my growing anxiety over how fast the plane was traveling and how close we were getting to the ground. "Oh? You often kiss strangers?"

"Only ones from Spain." So she'd nailed my heritage without even asking. Which seemed impossible, I was mostly half Spanish and German with a whole bunch of other things my mom couldn't seem to remember.

"Spain is for lovers," I found myself saying like an idiot.

She smiled, though.

And I wanted to think it was because of me, not because of who I was, or what I did.

"My favorite place in the world," she said in a faraway voice as the plane bounced lower, making her shriek as she clutched both my hands in hers. "Are we going to die?"

"Absolutely not," I lied. I wasn't sure what was going to happen, but I couldn't die, not when I finally had a fresh start. "We'll be just fine."

"Okay." She nodded a few times and gulped. "But just in case, I think I'll do this—"

Her mouth was on mine before I could protest.

And then any argument I would have had died on my lips at the first taste of her tongue. Her hands tugged on my hair as my arms wrapped around her warm body.

The plane made a screeching sound and then slammed against the runway, pulling us apart amidst sirens and cheers from the other passengers.

I stared at a pair of lips I wanted to taste again.

And when she said, "I'm Ashley, what's your name?"

I did the dumbest thing to date and lied. "I'm Hugo. Nice to meet you."

On behalf of 1001 Dark Nights,

Liz Berry and M.J. Rose would like to thank ~

Steve Berry
Doug Scofield
Kim Guidroz
Jillian Stein
Social Butterfly PR
Dan Slater
Asha Hossain
Chris Graham
Fedora Chen
Kasi Alexander
Jessica Johns
Dylan Stockton
Richard Blake
and Simon Lipskar

CPSIA information can be obtained
at www.ICGtesting.com
Printed in the USA
LVHW111821221019
634989LV00003B/383/P

9 781970 077131